The Wind Rose

The Wind Rose

The Prophecy Realized

Book Three of The Moon Singer

B. Roman

Prologue

"As this boy, now maturing into a man, meets opposition all around him, will he have the strength of faith and character to hold fast to his beliefs, to not be coerced by others to think his experience really is just an illusion?"

Other: When no one else has seen or heard what you have, it's difficult to hold on to a conviction. But, as we've stressed before, he must go deep within himself for that courage, to know that what he has witnessed is his own truth.

"But have I taken him as far as he is capable, or willing, to comprehend? Are we asking too much? Or should I do more?"

Other: You have done your part admirably. What you have helped him see will stay with him. Now it's up to him to experience the "knowing." That "knowing" is built upon the "Power of Three." Once he puts all the pieces together, the Three will become One.

"The *pieces* being the three sacred artifacts. Separately, they have their own individual power, but united the three synergize into One."

Other: Exactly. And when he discovers this, which he is so close to doing, his mission will be fulfilled.

"So, I shall stand back and let him move forward on his own intuition…"

Other: Oh, the things we can achieve when we aspire to the greatness within ourselves.

NASA Observatory

An opaque elliptical image with a glimmering outline soars across the evening sky then dissipates. Notice is taken by the night crew who dismiss it as an optical illusion. But its appearance is logged into the database of unusual sightings to be investigated.

Griffith Observatory

A translucent obelisk-shaped form moves out of the clouds, illuminating the starless mid-western sky. The night crew is breathlessly silent as the one obelisk becomes two, and then three, eerily linked together in one graceful motion. This uncanny vision, too, is noted into the sightings database just as it fades from view.

Port Avalon Observatory

A shimmering, lenticular cloud-shaped light glides across a part of the heavens almost too far away for the powerful telescope to perceive. Professor Ramirez squints hard trying to focus in on the faint image and determine what it is. Then he smiles broadly. He has seen it before, but just as before he will tell no one, not even his colleagues at the NASA and Griffith Observatories who have shared their sightings with him. This one he will keep to himself until the propitious moment.

One

Port Avalon

David Nickerson scans the diagram of an ancient compass into his computer then does a web search for it. In a few seconds, the words appear on the screen:

"Compass Rose, c 1770. *An early navigational aid. The Wind Rose was a compass without a magnetic needle, which had eight points named for the eight principal winds. Seafarers must have been able to tell the winds apart, by recognition of their temperature, moisture content, strength, or some other characteristic, or by association with the heavenly bodies, in order to use the Wind Rose effectively.*"

"Is that it?" David asks the machine incredulously, as though it will answer. "There has to be more. This thing blew up an entire continent!"

He searches further, using alternative key words and phrases. Nothing. "Maybe it's cryptic, or numerical" he guesses, and enters in some random numbers: 1, 2, 7, 5, 3 then hits the Enter key. Nothing.

The call indicator on David's TTY unit flashes. David types in "GA," signaling the Relay Operator to Go Ahead. It's Hannah, a member of the Beach Watch Team, reporting in on some unusual findings on the stretch of beach they've adopted.

Hannah picks up various items and describes them to David with distaste and chagrin. "We need to bring this up to the Town Council, David. Signs of industrial waste, trash from the tourists, erosion on the west cliff where they want to develop that thing for the Millennium celebration. Too delicate here."

The TTY Operator relays Hannah's message to him and the words dance across the fluorescent display board. David types a message back: "Okay, next meeting, we lay it on them."

The Beach Watch Team consists of students and political activists from Port Avalon's city college who are majoring in marine biology, geophysics, and meteorology. They are concerned about public access, over-development, beach erosion, litter and other issues along the 30-mile coast of Port Avalon that can potentially harm local wildlife and human quality of life.

David Nickerson, not yet 17, the youngest team member and also its founder, was inspired to organize The Beach Watch after reading tales of the "Watchers on the Headlands" of medieval times, who lit bonfires to alert townspeople of invaders approaching by sea. Today, the "watchers" carry hand-held computers and cell phones to communicate with each other and record their findings.

"Keep up the good work," David adds to the message. He then types in "SK" which tells the relay operator to Stop Keying, the conversation is over. Hannah's image disappears from the monitor.

When David returns his concentration to his computer screen, a strange message is displayed: "12 is 7 is 5 is 3."

"What the heck does that mean?" Tired, he dismisses it as gibberish and closes down his laptop for the day.

A flashing light on his desk alerts David that someone is coming into his room. His sister Sally enters, using her crutches deftly, moving with ease. This is an improvement over a wheelchair and leg braces, but not good enough for David who remembers how she danced with him without crutches at his birthday party. Or was that a dream? Sally seems not to remember it at all.

"Dad wants to talk to us," she signs to him.

Sally is now almost as good a signer as David, although he is the deaf one. David also reads lips expertly, and so they alternate forms of communication.

4

David's signed gesture is curt. "Not again. I don't think I can ever get him to understand."

"I'm not sure I do, any more."

"You of all people should understand." David's piercing blue eyes focus on Sally, silently urging her to remember that day on the beach two summers ago when their lives changed forever, all because of a supernatural crystal and an electrical storm.

"I did - about the Moon Singer and all, and even the Rose Crystal. I mean, look at me. Two years ago I couldn't even stand. Then I could. I know I regressed to braces and crutches, but it's better than a wheel chair. Your experiments with the crystals helped me so much. I believe something magical happens when you use them. But this other stuff about Mom is hard for me to absorb."

"Sal - it's the truth," David says, signing emphatically. "Every word of it. What good will it do to rehash it all. He believes me or he doesn't."

"He's worried about you. So am I."

"Well, don't be. I'm fine. Just frustrated."

"He's downstairs. There's someone with him."

"Who?"

Sally shrugs.

Isaac and Doctor Hilyer acknowledge David and Sally as they join them in the living room. As usual, Isaac speaks directly to David's face so his son can read his lips.

"Dr. Hilyer agreed to come here tonight and listen to your story. Perhaps he can help."

"What kind of doctor? A shrink? Come on, Dad. I'm not crazy." David's voice is now a maturing baritone, with little impediment. A stranger would never know he was completely deaf if they hadn't seen him sign.

Hilyer signs very little, so must add in some verbal conversation. "From what your father tells me, David, you've had quite an experience. It's caused you to become alienated from your family. An objective point of view might help clear things up."

David laughs cynically. "The only thing that will clear it up would be to make that ship appear again. Then you'd all have to believe me."

"The ship? You mean the ghost ship?"

"She's not a ghost ship," David snaps, his hand movements sharp. "She's real. But without the Singer, I'll never get her back. So what's the point."

"What's the *Singer*?"

"The crystal that conjured her up in the first place. But I lost it on Coronadus. So, there's nothing left to say." David flops down on a chair and leans back. He runs a quick hand through his dark blonde hair to get it out of his eyes.

"Where did you get this crystal, David?" Dr. Hilyer sits directly opposite him, leaning toward him in an attempt to gain David's confidence.

The psychiatrist's eyes are concerned, but a warm hazel brown, and were he not "the enemy" David just might like him. "My Aunt Dorothy gave it to me. She found it on one of her digs."

"I see. So this magic crystal is what started it all. Well, what if we tried some other crystals. Many of them have the same properties."

"NONE of them have what the Singer had."

"Tell me about your mother, David."

"She's dead."

Isaac Nickerson flinches at his son's bluntness. The feelings of guilt over the circumstances of Billie's death are still raw within him, the fact that he was driving the car when the accident happened. Billie died from her injuries and Sally was crippled.

"But you claim to have seen her, communicated with her," Dr. Hilyer says.

"I did. But I can't prove it."

"Without the Singer."

"Right."

The doctor reflects a bit. "Would you consider hypnosis? To help you remember things more clearly."

"I DO remember things clearly. I almost wish I didn't -" David stops, suddenly realizing that this might be what they have in mind. "No way. Uh - uh. Forget it. You're not going to wipe out my memories. Not with hypnosis, therapy, drugs, or a lobotomy. I know what I saw and I didn't imagine it! I'm out of here." Before Dr. Hilyer can reassure him that this is not his intent, David jumps out of the chair.

"David!" Isaac calls after his son as David stomps out the door.

Breaking into a sprint, David heads towards the village square where the hectic interaction of people, cars, buses and trucks refocuses his thoughts.

* * *

All around Port Avalon, construction is nearing completion for the Millennium celebration. It's an undertaking that has taken many months, but the town is determined to get a piece of the Millennium pie. This quaint seaside town, with a centuries-old history of shipbuilding, is emerging from a severe economic slump. All kinds of activities are being planned to lure wealthy VIPS: boat cruises, special commuter flights, galas, fancy dinners, and concerts, with ticket prices going as high as Super Bowl seats and promising to surpass them. New hotels are being erected on the coastline to house the thousands of new tourists who will come through on their trek across America to savor every festivity the momentous event has to offer.

Port Avalon has been booming ever since the news media covered the Children's Peace Flotilla, following David's return from Coronadus and his most startling transcendental experience. He *did* see his mother, there *is* a ship, there *was* a Singer crystal, and the Rose Crystal *could* make Sally walk normally again. It almost did, until Isaac inadvertently gave it away. Now all David has as evidence of his last adventure is the Wind Rose. But he must never let anyone know he has it. He promised Bianca - and his mother - he would guard it with his life. But why? What will he need it for? What good is it without the Singer?

Two

The young toughs close in on their prey, walking at a determined pace. Janice Cole hastens her step to get away from them, but she is wearing high heels and cannot walk fast enough. She tries to act fearless, or at least pretend not to know they are following her. Only a few more yards and she will be safe inside her car, on her way to the restaurant for her dinner date with her fiancé.

The beep of the remote key unlocking the car is their cue to pounce. Before Janice can open the door to safety, she is flung around and thrust against the left front fender. One thug holds her down, while the other struggles to get the keys from her hands.

"Let 'em go, bitch!" he yells, outraged that she is not cooperating.

Her instinct is to fight back, to try and gouge the thug's eyes out, but she is overpowered by a crushing blow to her face. The shocking pain causes her to relax her grip on the keys. She is pushed forcefully aside, and stumbles to the ground as the two assailants speed off in her car. From her coat pocket, Janice retrieves her cell phone and dials 911. Incredibly, it's busy! Frantically, she hits the speed dial and calls another number.

"Isaac here," he answers the call.

Janice tries to speak but all she can do is sob into the phone. "I – I - Isaac – "

"Who is this?" Isaac asks, then it clicks in. "Jan? Is that you? What's wrong? Are you all right? Jan?" Her sobbing has him frantic, too, but he calms her down enough to find out where she is. Knocking over his chair and spilling his glass of wine, Isaac rushes out of the restaurant and speeds off to Janice's side.

* * *

David, Dorothy and Sally sit impatiently in the ER waiting room while Isaac comforts Janice in the treatment room.

"How could this happen in our town," Dorothy steams. "What's happening to people?

"It's all these new tough kids moving in here from the city," Sally whines angrily. "They think they can terrorize us like they do where they come from. I hate it."

"It's what they call diversity," David says, cynically. "But it's really Millennium Madness. She shouldn't have been in that neighborhood anyway. Dumb."

"Stop it, David. Janice has had a terrifying experience," Dorothy chastises him. She signs emphatically, her arthritic fingers aching with each gesture. "Where is your compassion? Sometimes I think you're some other David, not my nephew."

David is almost contrite. "I think he's still somewhere out there, Aunt Dorothy. I haven't been able to find him myself."

Isaac appears and gives them an update. "She'll be fine. Physically. Those scum bags didn't break her jaw but her face is swollen and badly bruised. The doctors want to keep her overnight for observation. I'm going to stay here and wait for the trauma counselor."

"Can we see her?" Sally asks hopefully. She loves Janice, who is soon to be her stepmother. It was Janice whose loyalty and affection brought her father up from the brink of depression as well as financial ruin. Sally believes that wherever her mother is, she is happy that Isaac has found happiness and purpose again.

"She's sedated and sleeping now," Isaac says, "Tomorrow would be better."

Dorothy embraces her brother and shores him up. Sally kisses her Dad goodnight. David nods at his father, seemingly dispassionate, and strides briskly away, with his aunt and sister trailing behind him.

David loves Janice, too, and the thought of losing another mother figure in his life is too much to bear. First his real mother, Billie Nickerson, killed instantly in the car crash that crippled Sally. Then Bianca - who was so much like his mother he swears it was her spirit reincarnated – perishing in the cataclysmic destruction of Coronadus. And now Janice was almost ripped from his life in a senseless act of violence. No. He would not let them know that he cared. He would not even let himself think how much he cared.

Three

Bright and early the next morning, David arrives at his favorite place, the only place that gives him any feeling that he knows what his life is all about. The observatory sits atop the highest hill on the Port Avalon city college campus and affords a panoramic view of the city and a 10-mile stretch of the beautiful coastline. For a small town observatory, it boasts some of the most sophisticated meteorological equipment in the state, thanks to the lobbying and influence of Dr. Ramirez, David's idol and mentor. Together, David and the distinguished scholar spend countless hours exploring weather systems, having animated debates on religious and mythical symbolism as they relate to world weather conditions, and revel in a passion they both share: music.

But they don't just discuss the natural laws of music and how they parallel the natural laws of the Universe. David and Dr. Ramirez also jam a lot on Ramirez's triple bank of keyboards. With his new wireless hearing aid David can hear the higher frequencies of music, and the pulsing of the beat. And with a new computer program that he designed, he can actually see the notes and sound waves in living color on his computer screen.

"This is when I miss being able to hear the most," David confesses. "I so much want to hear all the music, the highs, the lows – all the subtleties."

"You hear *inner music*, David," Dr. Ramirez tells him. "It's probably more sublime than anything the human ear can experience." The miraculous invention of verbal texting allows David to read on a small monitor what Dr. Ramirez is saying as he speaks into his computer's mic.

"Do you think that musical vibrations can create life?" David asks.

Ramirez nods, used to such questions from David. "Create it, and destroy it."

"I remember you said that all life forms vibrate to a certain musical note. Even a blade of grass has its own frequency."

"Yes," Dr. Ramirez replies. He begins to play Chopin's *Eb Nocturne* providing a meditative background to his monologue. "Everything that moves, lives and breathes has its own frequency, its unique musical tone. As you recall, it was the Greek philosopher and mathematician Pythagoras who established the relationship between numbers and all universal manifestations – the circling of the planets, the lunar cycle, the rhythm of the tides, the growth cycles of plant and animal life. His geometric formulas formed the basis for the seven- and twelve-note scales and tonic systems that are the foundation of the music of the Great Masters."

"Beethoven, Mozart, Bach..."

"To name a few," Dr. Ramirez says. "Pythagoras believed if these numerical formulas were used in the composition of music, the sound vibrations would resonate in harmony with universal forces and enhance life physically, emotionally, and spiritually. He believed that music had divine properties. If its formulas were used unwisely or incorrectly, chaos would result in the universe."

"Chaos?" David ponders.

"Chaos in the soul, in society, and in the forces of nature."

David is dying to ask Dr. Ramirez if he knows anything about the Wind Rose compass and its ability to cause catastrophic damage in the environment, but he dares not even mention it. He must never mention it to anyone, ever, as Bianca had made him promise.

Nor does David want to reveal that the only reason he founded Beach Watch was in the hope that he would somehow be able to summon up the clipper ship Moon Singer with the Wind Rose, or miraculously find the Singer crystal washed up on the shore. Instead he keeps the conversation focused on the ecological conditions that affect Port Avalon.

Later, when David leaves Dr. Ramirez's observatory studio, he does not see the message on the computer screen that pops ups again: "12 is 7 is 5 is 3."

Four

"Let me tell you, good people, and hear me, hear me. Our eternity with God is going to be awesome, so awesome I can't even describe it." The Reverend Jedediah Holmsby is 45 minutes into his sermon, working up a sweat proselytizing on the imminent coming of Christ. "And it's going to happen soon."

The congregation of the Holy Converted Church of Port Avalon needs no convincing. Heads nod. Several people call out, "Amen!"

Reverend Holmsby pulls a white linen handkerchief from the pocket of his dark blue suit and dabs his forehead. He waves his Bible in the air.

"There's no need to call the psychic hot line, or cruise the web. God has revealed it, the end of the planet Earth, and it's all right here in the scriptures. In the Gospel According to Luke, Jesus said: There will be signs in the sun, the moon, the stars. And on the Earth, distress among nations confused by the roaring of the sea and the waves. People will faint from fear and foreboding of what is coming upon the world, for the powers of the heavens will be shaken."

On cue, a chorus of 50, wearing perfectly-tailored gold-trimmed ruby red robes, elevate the room with their powerful voices and soul-stirring gospel music. The church congregation waves its arms to the heavens, shouting awed and reverent Hallelujahs.

* * *

That evening, the Astronomy Club of Port Avalon University is convened atop Vista Point. Some never-before seen vision causes Jeff, one of the fledgling astronomers, to take special note.

"What's this, Joe?" Jeff relinquishes the telescope to his colleague.

Joe studies the celestial object pensively. "You mean that triangle-shaped thing?"

"Well, that's a scientific description if I ever heard one," Jeff cracks. "But, yeah, that triangle-shaped thing. Is it a light or a solid object?"

"Hard to tell," Joe replies. "It keeps ducking behind the clouds. It's moving fast, I'll tell you that."

"Can we get a picture?"

"I don't know if the camera will pick it up, but let's give it a try."

Joe aims his telephoto lens at the mysterious object in the heavens. His camera clicks numerous times in succession, taking multiple images in split second sequence. When the object disappears into the cosmos, Joe checks the digital images.

"Well, I didn't think I'd get much of anything," Joe says. "But there's something there all right."

"It's kind of blurry because it's moving so fast," Jeff comments.

Joe shakes his head, bewildered. "I don't think it's blur. It's more of a shimmer. There's a glow coming from - whatever it is."

"Well, if ships could fly," Jeff laughs, "I'd say it was a ship. Like an old fashioned clipper."

"Like the Flying Dutchman? That legendary Ghost ship that can never make port?"

"In this case, a ship that can never find a planet to land on. Wonder how long it's been up there?"

* * *

Religious fundamentalism, doomsday prophecies, and all manner of superstition surrounding the coming millennium are rich fodder for every medium, even on local Port Avalon television talk shows. Psychiatrist Dr. Hilyer, who is also an expert on religion and mythology, is a frequent guest on such programs where the host, this time Randy Phillips, poses the same questions over and over:

"The dramatic increase in Apocalyptic fervor is quite disturbing, Dr. Hilyer," Phillips asserts. "Is this hysteria the norm around an approaching millennium, or is there really something to these doomsday prophecies?"

"Yes, it is the norm," Hilyer replies, "especially when approaching a historic point in time. Most of the doomsday prophecies fall into the category of Scriptures known as Apocalypses, which were written during times of oppression to reassure persecuted believers that God had not forgotten them. However, apocalypses portrayed divine intervention in a distant, cosmic future, and were not meant to be taken literally."

"So, are you saying that today's self-anointed prophets are harmless?" the host asks a loaded question.

"Not exactly. The obsession with equating current events with Biblical prophecies causes more harm than good, especially when they put their own interpretation on things. By assigning hero and villain roles, they fuel distrust and even hatred of public officials and institutions, and increase the expectations of an end-times assault by demonic forces. There are many such examples that are now part of history."

"Like the Branch Davidians, under the leadership of self-proclaimed prophet David Koresh, whose killing of federal agents ignited the Waco catastrophe?"

"Yes," Hilyer concurs. "One result of this was to ignite a violent response from avowed government hater Timothy McVeigh who was transformed psychologically by the standoff, and who ultimately bombed the Oklahoma City federal building in retaliation two years later. Sadly, other such incidents followed, as we know."

"And lest we forget," Phillips adds, "there have also been mass suicides by cults who actually desired to accelerate the end times, such as the Jonestown tragedy in Guyana and the Heaven's Gate suicide near San Diego, California."

"There is a slight difference here, though," Hilyer clarifies. "Jim Jones, founder of the People's Temple in Jonestown, was a deranged drug abuser who exacted control over a group of people living in a primitive, agricultural community by using fearful biblical connotations, and the group succumbed to his brutal programming by drinking poison.

"The Heaven's Gate cult consisted of highly intelligent, computer web designers who cultivated members and spread their information through the internet. The Heaven's Gate leaders were also deranged, but claimed to have arrived on Earth via a UFO and would return to their source by riding the tale of the Hale Bop Comet which was due to pass by at a specific point in time. Amazingly, they enticed several dozen people to agree to a murder-suicide pact as the means to experience the Rapture."

"So, a computer savvy civilization is no assurance of an enlightened civilization," Phillips posits grimly.

"No, and I expect there will be more such conspiratorial doomsday predictions in the coming years, whether it's the fear of a killer asteroid, a collision with another planet or with the supposed end of the Mayan calendar."

"But give us some hope here, Doctor," Phillips implores. "Must the apocalypse be strictly a doomsday event? Could there be a healing power of the apocalypse?"

"Yes, indeed," Hilyer asserts optimistically. "Interpreted positively, the apocalyptic vision metaphorically represents the death of suffering and the rebirth of joy. It is truly meant to give us hope that, despite considerable evidence to the contrary, in the end it is GOOD that will prevail. It is hope, after all, that makes it possible for us to live day after day."

Five

Janice removes her dark glasses to reveal the bluish bruises under her eyes that are a constant reminder of the attack she suffered a few days earlier. Though ready and willing to press charges and withstand a public trial, she was unable to positively identify the toughs who carjacked her. It was night, their faces were in shadows, their clothing was dark, their hands were strong and rough. They were boys, however. That she did know, by their voices. Older teens, but still boys. Her car was found the next morning stripped and abandoned on a side road leading out of town, and the case was chalked up to random gang violence.

Aunt Dorothy touches Janice's arm compassionately. "I'm just so sorry for what you went through, Janice. You know this is not what Port Avalon is about. We won't tolerate hate and violence here," Dorothy affirms.

"I appreciate that, Dorothy. But tonight, let's talk about more pleasant things."

"You finally kept our dinner date," Isaac says, trying to be lighthearted. He had wanted to find the thugs himself and beat them to within an inch of their lives. "The good news is we are finally here to celebrate our engagement."

The entire family is at the table, the same table in the same restaurant on Lighthouse Point where they all convened to celebrate David's 16th birthday and graduation some months earlier.

"Let's make a pact that whenever we have good things to celebrate, it will always be here," Sally suggests.

"If we can keep these two from talking about work," Dorothy teases Isaac and Janice, both renowned workaholics.

"Well, it's hard not to revel in the economic resurgence of Port Avalon. Not to mention the raising of Cole Shipping from the economic grave yard," Isaac boasts. "And I just can't wait to see the country stand up and take notice when we launch the Millennium Miracle Ship."

The brainchild and "baby" of Isaac Nickerson and Cole Shipping, the Millennium Miracle Ship will travel the world bringing medical care and educational tools to the poor, sick, and disenfranchised people of all nations who need them.

In a fervent and unrelenting solicitation campaign, Isaac and Janice had pulled in four million dollars' worth of pledges in the form of cash, supplies, and services from philanthropic organizations worldwide. That would barely cover a one-year tour, but Isaac and Janice both felt confident that the project would be supported well beyond that.

Throughout dinner, David has been distant and somewhat petulant. He recalls the previous dinner party celebration as one of the happiest of his life. It was a milestone for him in graduating at the head of his class a year earlier than the other students because of his innovative computer skills, and getting that Blue touring car, an exact replica of the one in his Coronadus adventure - or was it his illusion? - and seeing Sally dance again, without her crutches or braces. Or was that an illusion, too, like his communicating with his dead mother? No, not for David. The others may not believe him – Dad, Dr. Hilyer, even Sally who once believed everything David said. But David knows the truth. It was real.

As the family chatters and reminisces happily, beautiful music begins to emanate from the Mermaid's harp as she glides serenely by their table. Seeing her atop the automated faux lily pad floating in the restaurant's decorative pond, it is a moment of *déjà vu* for David, a recollection of that memorable night when he could actually hear the music, and no one knew he could, except Sally...

"Do you hear that song?" David had signed to his sister inconspicuously.

She nodded and signed back, "It's the mermaid singing." Then, with a start she asked him, "David, can you -?"

David had put his fingers to his lips to silence her.

Sally signed discreetly, "Can you hear her?"

"I hear something - music that I've heard before. What is it?"

"I don't recognize it, yet I do. Wait. I'll find out."

Trying to be nonchalant, Sally asked the others at the table if they knew the name of the song the mermaid was singing.

Isaac thought a moment but couldn't place it.

"It's an old song, I know," Janice said. "But the title escapes me."

"Fascination," Dorothy told them. "You know. The waltz. '*It was fascination, I know,*'" she sang.

"Oh, yes." They had all nodded in agreement, and then continued their animated conversation, filling the air with joyous laughter.

But Sally knew it was not that old song, that it was something else. "Something mysterious and magical, isn't it?" she signed to her brother, and he nodded.

The biggest shock had come when David got a closer look at the Mermaid. She was strikingly lovely, identical in every way to the beautiful young girl he had fallen in love with, with the same golden hair cascading softly over her shoulders almost to her waist, and the same full, inviting, yet forbidden, lips.

Then he saw the pendant around her neck. It glistened in the spotlight, a beautiful Rose Crystal pendant just like the one he had brought back from the Island of Darkness after it become the Kingdom of Light once again, and gave to Sally.

"*It can't be. It just looks like it,*" he had thought then.

And when the music had resonated from the Mermaid's golden harp and the words flowed from her full, soft mouth... "*Moon Singer, Moon Singer, take to the sea, fly on the wind where the sky used to be...*" David knew it was her. *Saliana! Princess Saliana.* Astonished and delighted beyond belief, David had risen slightly from his chair to acknowledge her, but just as magically as she had appeared, Saliana transformed back into the restaurant's performer again, older, with dark hair instead of golden.

"David?" Dorothy had taken his hand in concern. "Are you all right? Too much dessert?" she joked, in her usual lighthearted manner.

"Uh, yeah. I'm stuffed. Um, Sally?" he said, turning then to his sister, "would you like to dance with me?"

Sally's eyes widened. She hadn't danced since before the accident. "Dance? With these?" She motioned to her crutches, propped against her chair.

"It's okay. I'm strong enough to hold you." David helped Sally to the dance floor as Isaac, Dorothy and Janice watched, dumbfounded. As if on cue, the Mermaid had taken a break from her harp playing and popular music had begun to pulsate from the overhead speakers.

Alternately signing and speaking, Sally and David conducted a secretive conversation, while smiling and pretending casualness. All this, while trying to maneuver on the dance floor, was the kind of challenge both siblings loved.

"Sally, whatever happened to the Rose Crystal Pendant I gave you?" David asked.

"It's gone, David. Daddy gave it away to some charity when he donated the rest of Mama's things."

David's heart had sunk at the loss. "Why did he do that!"

"It was an accident. I put the pendant in one of Mama's jewelry boxes and Daddy picked it up without looking inside. I went to look for it last week and it was gone."

"I think I know where it went." David's eyes searched for the Mermaid.

"Really?" Sally pleaded, "Oh, please get it back for me!"

"I'll try. If the person who has it will part with it."

"Oh, David. Keep dancing with me. Here comes one of my favorite ballads. Can you feel the beat?"

David picked up on the rhythm quickly as Sally swayed in his arms. He was thrilled to see his sister's eyes light up as she danced again, even though he mostly carried her weight.

Soon, Sally was lost in the music, her gaze far away in a fantasy where the handsome prince glided on the dance floor with his beautiful princess. The crutches were no hindrance to her movements; they seemed not to exist at all. Refusing to accept her disability as a reality, her body followed her spirit's lead.

When the Mermaid had taken her place again on the lily pad, and gently plucked the strings on her harp, the Rose Crystal Pendant emanated a magical radiance until only its glow was seen, only its transcendent energy was felt. Sally's crutches fell away and she pirouetted with arms outstretched, free and elegantly alone...

"David. David where are you?" Isaac calls pleasantly across the table, trying to penetrate that faraway look in his son's eyes. "It's time to go."

"Huh? Oh - oh, yeah. Sure." His mind now snapping back to the present moment, David scoots his chair away from the table and stands. He reaches over to pull Sally's chair out and help her up. Reality intrudes on his happy reverie that Sally had been healed and could walk and dance unaided, and his mood darkens again.

Six

At home later, Isaac confronts David about his moodiness almost ruining the celebration of his and Janice's engagement. "I'm telling you now, David, if you don't agree to see Dr. Hilyer voluntarily, I'll take steps to make you do it."

"You can't force me, Dad," David yells. "I'm old enough to make my own decisions."

"Well, the decisions you are making lately are not those of a mature young man. And while you're under my roof, you'll do as I say!"

"Well, then, I'll get out from under your roof!"

"Don't be ridiculous. This is your home. I don't want you to leave, David. I just want you to -"

"To what? Do as you say? Be what you want me to be? What you *approve* of?"

"What's that supposed to mean?" Isaac snaps, defensively.

"You know what I mean. You never accepted the fact that I'm different. Ever since I went deaf you refused to accept me as I am."

Isaac is heart stricken. "That's not true and you know it."

"Do I? Why did you never like me to sign or even learn to read lips? Always pushing medications and vitamins and surgeries on me."

"I wanted you to get well. To hear again. Is that so wrong?" he pleads with his son.

"No. You wanted me to be perfect!"

"That's ridiculous. And unfair."

"But it's true. Mom was the only one who accepted me, who helped me accept myself. Until you killed her!"

Isaac is crushed by this accusation. A knife through his heart from his own son. He thought they had resolved the issue of the accident that killed his wife, David and Sally's beloved mother. He sinks into a chair, all the energy drained from his face and body.

"The truth is, David," Isaac confesses with a weary voice, "I felt guilty for your deafness. You inherited the gene from me. It runs in my family and yet I never was affected. It skipped me and inflicted you instead." His voice picking up energy, Isaac emphasizes, "That's why I wanted to do everything to get you well!"

"Your way! Without giving me the chance to decide for myself what I want, what kind of treatment, if any, I want!"

"That's the problem," Isaac bellows. "You don't want any treatment. It makes no sense at all!"

The yelling and fighting are more than Dorothy can stand and she storms into the living room to confront them.

"Stop it, both of you. Isaac, you're being rigid and narrow-minded. And David, you're being disrespectful. And that, I won't tolerate. I love you both so much – and – and – an -"

Dorothy's speech suddenly slurs and a panicked expression fills her eyes. The right side of her face droops sadly downward, and her right knee buckles, dragging her down to the floor.

"Dorothy! What is it!" Isaac and David both grab her and support her to the couch. All she can do is make indistinguishable utterances.

"Dad! What's wrong? What do we do?"

"I think she's having a stroke. I'll call 911."

Seven

Paralyzed on her right side, with her left side mildly affected, Dorothy's prognosis is only fair. She could regain some, but not all, of her motor skills with medication and extensive therapy, according to the doctors. But, after a few days in the hospital, Dorothy insists on coming home for rehabilitation. The family rallies around her, happy she is once again in familiar surroundings, and for a few days there are no fights, no conflicts. The Nickerson family bonds together as they once did in happier times, in their love for each other.

As always, David yearns to converse with his aunt and visits her in her room, which was once his own room, on the third floor of the Nickerson house, with its expansive view of the ocean and the family cemetery. Situated cliffside at the far end of the property, adorned by uniquely shaped cypress trees, is his mother's grave watched over eternally by the marble angel that came to life one fateful day... or did David just imagine that, too, like all the other bizarre incidents everyone thinks he has hallucinated?

The nurse has just finished bathing Dorothy and combing her silver hair. At the sight of David, Dorothy's eyes light up and she smiles, a bit of color coming back to her cheeks. Pleased that her patient is comforted, the nurse leaves the two of them alone.

Dorothy cannot speak clearly, but she can sign with a shaky left hand. "Hello, my dearest nephew," she moves her fingers slowly but correctly. "Why the sad face?"

"You always wanted this room," David reminds her, "but this is not how I want you to have it. I hate seeing you like this. If I hadn't messed up so much with Dad this wouldn't have happened."

"Not your fault. Just life."

"Aunt Dorothy, I never did tell you everything about the Moon Singer. I kept getting sidetracked."

"I know. Me, too," she signs. "Tell me now. I have nothing – but time."

David straddles the hardback chair next to Dorothy's bed, and rests his arms on the back of it.

"Remember when you suggested I try to communicate with Mom, tell her what I was feeling, all the hurt and anger over her being gone? Well, I went to her grave. I took the crystals like you told me. I used them the same as I did the first time, and I had another - another adventure - only this time I didn't go to the Island of Darkness, I went to a strange city called Coronadus.

"So many things happened there. There was a woman who was very powerful. She believed in a lot of the things Mom believed in. She looked just like Mom. I - I think she *was* Mom."

Outside Dorothy's room, Isaac and Sally overhear David's conversation with his aunt, and the preposterous story he is telling her. Isaac is furious and when David comes out of Dorothy's room, he confronts his son, pulling him by the arm out of Dorothy's earshot.

"I don't appreciate you eavesdropping," David snaps, the animosity returning.

"I wasn't. Sally and I just happened to come up to see Dorothy and heard you. What kind of craziness is this – adventures, crystals, Island of Darkness. And seeing some woman who you believe is your mother? What's got into you, David?"

"It's all true, and Sally knows it. Tell him, Sal. Tell him that you know."

"Oh, David. I've stuck by you and I believe everything, except..." She starts to cry, "...except the part about Mom. I don't know why, but I'm scared to believe it."

"Yet you believe all that other silliness?" Isaac fumes in exasperation. "I don't know about you two." Clearly in conflict, Sally goes to her room and closes the door.

"I wish you would talk to Dr. Hilyer, David. You're irrational."

"But, Dad," David implores, "don't you think it's possible that there are other places, other dimensions beyond this one? That we can communicate with people from other worlds?"

"Men have been trying for hundreds of years," Isaac says, emphatically, "and no one has been successful. There are no UFO's or ET's."

"I'm not talking about aliens or other planets, Dad. I mean people like us but in another time and place – the afterlife, maybe, or a parallel universe…"

"David. What's happening between us? We used to be so close. You've changed so much. I hardly know you anymore." Deflated, Isaac shakes his head and retires to his room.

"Dad, when you've been through what I've been through, it definitely changes you," David calls after him, but Isaac is behind the closed door and does not hear him.

Back in his aunt's room, David takes her hand. Though she can't say the words, the look in Dorothy's eyes speaks volumes of love for him.

"I know you believe me, Aunt Dorothy. And I promise you I will find a way to prove it to everyone else. And I'll find something to make you well again, the same way that Sally walked again. And this time, I'll do it right."

Eight

David works at his computer with single-minded focus trying to design gridwork patterns that will recreate the energy of the Singer and Rose crystals. Each time he puts together a grid, he receives a computer message instead, each one more cryptic than the previous one:

"There will be no star wars in the next millennium. No one will have to fight to touch the stars or claim them as their own"... *"There is no ultimate truth, for the Universe is constantly revealing itself and all its mysteries, which are infinite and unknowable."*

But one elaborate grid pattern evokes a message that is chillingly akin to what Ishtar once told him:

"Humanity should always be greater than technology."

At this, the hard drive crashes and the monitor goes dark.

David wonders if the problem is evidence of the century-end computer glitch that everyone fearfully anticipates because computers were never programmed to numerically recognize a new century let alone a new millennium. Computers run everything from trains to nuclear power plants to bank systems, to milking cows and running the White House. At the stroke of midnight on December 31, the theory goes, all computers and all systems run by computers will fail completely, with disastrous results worldwide. For several years, computer programmers have been working at a feverish pitch to correct old encoding systems in computers that impact financial, political, social and business structures.

But David's computer is a new model with a fail-safe encoding system built in. No, it's not the Millennium bug.

"What are you trying to tell me?" he demands, and swats the monitor with an open hand.

A vivid memory springs to David's mind, of his adventure on Coronadus when all of the machines came back to life after lying dormant for years. Coronadus had once been a teeming metropolis of scientific and technological sophistication and innovation. But all the knowledge was used for self-aggrandizement, power, and military aggression. When finally the psyche of Coronadus lost its ability to distinguish between what was morally right and what was profitable, a catastrophic war nearly destroyed the entire civilization.

For years after, Coronadans lived simply, rejecting any and all technology, happy in the stillness and serenity of the organic life – until David arrived with the Singer crystal that reactivated the dormant industrial relics of the pre-war society. Not only did all the machines and electrical power systems re-awaken, so did the Coronadans' lust for power and material things.

Now David realizes that one important thing was missing from the Coronadus culture: music. Except for a strolling minstrel or two in the town square, there was nothing in that majestic city that supported any art forms at all, no galleries or theaters, no concert halls or music conservatories. As David had always heard from Dr. Ramirez, "the measure of a great civilization is the value it places on the arts." Music is the source of all life, of all things sustainable, he believed, "possessing a divinity everyone should experience."

Maybe, like the Coronadans, I have to go back to the beginning, to the place where things were simpler." David muses. Then maybe I'll find the solution to my own problems.

Nine

As David and Dr. Ramirez study the weather systems
around the country, the forecast looks favorable for the coming
weeks. But an unusual wind system hovers over the Port Avalon area
of the satellite map.

"This is really strange." Dr. Ramirez's comment streams across
David's screen in red letters.

"What is?" David sends an instant reply.

"I tested the vibrational frequency of Port Avalon this morning,"
the doctor replies, "and it resonated to F# Major, a very calm earth
frequency. Now, this disruption in the weather. Something is out of
tune in the universe."

David looks up from his monitor with a perplexed expression. With
Dr. Ramirez, dissonance in music also means chaos in the world. It is
a reflection of man's moods, his consciousness. The professor openly
harbors animosity toward contemporary music and believes it is in
large part a cause of the unrest, violence and disruptive behavior in
society.

He once recalled to David what a respected music icon had said in
a recent magazine interview: "The music industry is a cesspool. I'm
ashamed to be a part of it. The videos, especially, have corrupted our
children. The way the girl singers dress, the obscene gestures on stage,
it's soft porn. Behind the scenes it's overrun with greed, drugs, and
untalented and unprincipled thugs."

"Come on, Doc," David had protested. "Everyone in the music biz can't be a corrupt thug."

"Not everyone *in* music, David, just the people who run the business. The power brokers. We are at their mercy."

Sounds like Nathan Fischbacher and his greedy corporate cronies, David ruminated. Fischbacher, the snake of a businessman who once ran Cole Shipping, stole his father's designs, and almost swindled the town of Port Avalon out of their economic livelihood. People in power. Must they always be evil? David hoped it wasn't true.

* * *

Even in the fall, Port Avalon's weather is usually mild, never stormy. But as though validating Dr. Ramirez's concerns about something being amiss in the universe, the clear blue sky suddenly turns black and foreboding. The sight triggers anxiety in David and he quickly leaves his computer station to stand close to the observatory's panoramic windows. Without warning, a wild palm frond flies into the window. Instinctively David ducks, forgetting that the windows are double-paned and virtually unbreakable. Still, the shock of the flying debris unnerves him, especially when another frond and other objects sail by in quick succession.

For 20 minutes a sustained wind of 60 miles per hour pounds the coastal town, bringing with it a blinding rain that dumps six inches of water, overflows in ditches and sweeps onto heavily trafficked roads. Fender benders abound, and one major accident sends four people to the hospital in critical condition. Numerous trees topple, bringing down power lines with them as they crash onto homes and cars. Then, as suddenly as it came, the storm abates. The sky is again that beautiful serene cloudless blue typical of Port Avalon in the autumn.

"Dr. Ramirez! What's going on?" David beseeches the professor. "How can this be happening!" David turns toward Ramirez hoping for an explanation, but sees him slumped on the floor next to his chair.

"Doc? Doc!" David calls, checking the man's pulse. Ramirez is white and his skin clammy. "I'll call 911!"

But the professor comes to and shakes his head no, stopping David from calling, saying that he is alright.

"I really think I should call someone. You look awful. What happened?"

"I'm not sure," Dr. Ramirez says, as David helps him up and into his chair. "I was just entering some data and, well - I just blacked out, I guess."

"Yeah. You and the sky," David quips.

"What do you mean? The sky looks fine, David. Clear and calm."

"It wasn't that way a minute ago. Listen. I think you'd better go home. Do you want me to drive you?"

"No. No. Thanks, David. I'm okay now." He sips some mineral water from the ever-present sports bottle on his desk. "There. That's better. Thanks. But I will go home early. You should, too."

"I'll be leaving in a minute," David says. "I just have to close down our stations."

Ramirez leaves the lab, but David decides to follow after him just to be sure he's really okay. David turns off his computer, then goes to the professor's station. A dizzying string of mysterious codes on Ramirez's screen disappear swiftly as David shuts the system down.

Ten

Dr. Ramirez's house is on the same route as David's. Once he is certain that the professor has arrived safely, David drives home to be sure that everyone there is okay. Aside from a mess of small tree branches in the front yard and some overturned flower pots on the porch, the Nickerson house seems to be untouched by the storm. He jogs up the stairs to check on Dorothy. She is sound asleep with her nurse in the room reading. Isaac is at a meeting, the nurse tells him, and Sally is at a friend's house.

David decides to evaluate the damage done to the ecosystem on the beach. He finds a lot of kelp, dead jellies and starfish littering the sand. Large slabs of wood, pieces of pipe and roof shingles lay in a disturbing heap on the once pristine sand.

Heather is there, and she rushes to his side, instinctively about to give him a hug. Surprised by the gesture, David stiffens and pulls back from her.

"David," she signs. "I was so worried about you. I'm glad you're okay." Heather loves David and longs for an indication from him that he feels the same. She learned sign language in the hopes it would bring them closer, and educated herself on the use of technical equipment designed for the hearing impaired. David respects and cares for Heather, and enjoys sharing their passion for the Beach Watch program, but for reasons she cannot understand, he resists anything more than a platonic relationship.

Heather catches David's eye and says, "There's going to be a meeting of the Beach Watch members tonight at seven. Can you come?"

"Sure. What's the agenda?"

"The storm, for one," she says. "And the effects of all the new development on Port Avalon's coastline. We're preparing for the next City Council meeting."

David nods. "I'll be there."

"Well...I have to go now," Heather says, hoping David will go with her.

"See ya later," David waves her off casually, and Heather backs away a few steps, reluctant to leave. Seeing the far-away look in his eyes, a look she has seen before but could never penetrate, she turns and leaves, disappointed as usual.

When he is certain Heather is out of sight, David removes the Wind Rose from his pants pocket. He had sensed something was happening but he didn't dare reveal the compass in front of Heather. Bianca had told him never to let anyone know he had it, and he kept his promise faithfully. It is as he thought. The needle is spinning on the antique navigational instrument, spinning like it had in Coronadus when it caught the magnetic field of the Singer crystal David carried in the pouch on his belt.

It can only mean one thing. The spin of the needle on the Wind Rose means that the Singer is near, and so is the great ship Moon Singer. A small rogue wave washes over David's feet and when the tide ebbs something glints in the sand. Its brilliance is unmistakable. It *is* the Singer. It is the *Singer*! Desperately, David reaches for it but it eludes his grasp as another wave splashes over it. The breaker pulls the Singer out of the sand and into the receding water.

Frantic, David wades into the surf to retrieve the crystal, but he isn't fast enough. The strong pull of the tide carries the Singer out to the open sea. David is devastated yet elated at the same time. He now knows the Singer is not lost forever. He will get it back. But how? And when? And when he does get it back, what in the world will he do with it? At the moment, he has no mission, no reason to possess it.

Not at this moment, anyway. Is his life about to be disrupted again? Does he really want it to be?

Eleven

The members of the Beach Watch Team wait impatiently for their turn on the City Council Agenda while some mundane township business is discussed and entered into record. The Team had voted unanimously the night before to bring their issues immediately to the Council and the public, and hope to have ample time to present their case. Heather takes the podium as spokesperson with an articulate and confident demeanor.

"The brief but powerful storm Port Avalon experienced yesterday gave us a glimpse of our lack of readiness to handle a severe emergency," Heather proclaims. "The mess on the beach will take days to clean up, and a lot of the debris out there came from uncontained building materials and hazardous chemicals used in constructing all those ostentatious exhibits for the Millennium celebration."

"Miss Du Priest," Councilman Jergens addresses Heather, with a patronizing lilt to his voice, "Port Avalon needs those ostentatious exhibits as you call them to further ensure the economic livelihood of the town. The more visitors we can bring in for the celebration, the more money we'll have to fund those projects that you and your team so ardently embrace."

"Yes," Heather agreed, "more money for the right kind of projects would be welcome, but not if your contractors cause more problems than we already have."

"Problems is an understatement," Jim Dancy interrupts from the audience. "What's the Town Council gonna do about all the immigrants coming here to take over jobs that we locals are supposed to have? All the construction and landscaping, the craftsman's jobs we could do just as well. But we won't work for peanuts."

Jim Dancy had made a similar argument a year ago when Port Avalon was contemplating taking on a Navy contract to build war ships. Only then, his concern was government employees coming in to fill the jobs that the local residents needed desperately.

Feeling Jim's frustration, several constituents grumble along with him. Mayor Fiori bangs his gavel loudly several times for order.

"Okay, everyone," the Mayor imposes, "the jobs issue is not on the agenda tonight. You'll have to sign up with the Court Clerk to be heard on that."

"We'll be heard all right," Jim counters, "by you and the unwelcome out-of-towners who don't belong here..."

Mayor Fiore is exasperated. "Jim, that's enough of that kind of talk. You try my patience and your remarks are incendiary. Bring it to the Court Clerk for a proper hearing."

"If I may continue?" Heather beseeches the panel.

"Yes, Miss Du Priest. You have the floor, but make it quick."

"The Beach Watch Team is here tonight to give you a wake-up call. If this storm is a harbinger, we all must be prepared."

"I have to agree with Miss Du Priest on this," Councilman Deitz says. "We have a Disaster Preparedness Plan that will be a disaster if we don't vote soon on funds to reinforce the levee just north of town. A levee break would be catastrophic if an even bigger storm comes through here."

Councilman Jergens, who is the tight-fisted fiscal officer on the Council, differs. "Even with the revenue from new development, we can't make the levee a priority right now. Our funds are primarily allocated in the short term for grants to local businesses to upgrade for the Millennium Project, a policy I might add agreed to by the Council with the full support of the citizens."

"I'll tell you one way to raise more revenue," Heather submits adamantly. "Levy heavy fines on the developers for any damage they inflict on the ecosystem. In fact, let them post a bond in front held in escrow for just such a purpose."

The Beach Watch Team applauds enthusiastically, but their outburst is waved off by the mayor who counters with, "That would only discourage growth and limit the town's potential in the free market."

"We are not anti-growth," Heather implores, gesturing out towards the Team. "But with growth comes responsibility. We are the stewards of the Earth, not the custodians of a sewer. The reason people visit Port Avalon and want to live here is because we still have one of the few unspoiled beaches left in the country. We have protected marine life habitats and fascinating tide pools teaming with organisms vital to the health of the environment. They want this more than more high rise hotels and shopping malls."

"Or short term residents who steal our jobs then take the money and run," Jim Dancy pops up again.

With the meeting going overtime and getting out of control, a motion is made to adjourn, tabling the Beach Watch's issues. The motion is seconded, and carried, but the grumbling of disgruntled Port Avalon citizens follows them from the Council chambers and into the street.

Throughout the entire proceeding, David has sat quietly, reading lips and absorbing the sign language provided by an interpreter. A year ago, he was not so dispassionate, when the town voted to accept the contract from the Navy.

He was livid and disheartened to envision the drastic change that would come over Port Avalon. But because some dedicated and innovative children in the town came up with alternative ideas on how to make Port Avalon prosperous using creative ideas and peaceful solutions, the Navy contract wasn't needed.

For a while Port Avalon reveled in the influx of new business from people all over the country who sought out the town's hospitable and warm environment. Then it happened, the Millennium Madness, as

David named it, the desire for more money and bigger commercial enterprises, all fueled by unfounded paranoia.

David isn't too concerned about Jim Dancy's fury over the immigrant population, for it was Jim Dancy who had made the most startling turnaround a year ago, becoming a kind and selfless neighbor. Had Jim not used his pickup truck to haul in a new storage freezer for Maggie Sturgess' restaurant, she would have had to shut down indefinitely. Maggie rewarded Jim with a month of free meals for saving her business. David believes Jim will come around again this time, for the good of all concerned.

Twelve

David unties the rope of the dinghy from its moorings in the estuary, steps in and rows a few hundred yards out into the calm ocean. He opens his laptop and boots it up, and places the Wind Rose compass on the seat beside him. If he can recreate the Star of David grid pattern in his computer, he just might be able to conjure up the clipper ship Moon Singer, the way he did before.

On that first day of summer more than a year ago David had used his prized crystal collection to form the sacred Star of David grid, placing the Singer crystal at the apex of the dominant triangle. Back then, he didn't have a clue as to what he was doing. It was just a fun experiment. He had used a twig to draw a triangle in the sand, then an inverted triangle over that one, then laid the crystals strategically on the wet sand to make the six-pointed Star of David energy formation. He hadn't known then that the double pyramid design was extremely powerful for elevating one's consciousness, and for facilitating inter-dimensional journeying.

His sister was with him that day, watching with fascination from her wheelchair. She worried that he might get hurt from the experiment, especially since an electrical storm was brewing. But that's just what David was hoping for, a bolt of lightning to strike the crystals and energize them to do something amazing.

And when the lightening finally did strike the Singer, the little crystal acted as a conduit and transmitted its power to each and every other crystal in the grid. The force was so potent that it knocked David unconscious. When he awoke, Sally was gone, her wheelchair empty. And before his eyes, floating majestically on the water, was the mystical clipper ship, Moon Singer, waiting to transport David away on his first adventure: to find his sister Sally.

But today, David must rely on technology to recreate the experiment. Today, there is no storm brewing, and no Singer crystal, the amazing artifact that can sing the mysteries of the universe and confer on its owner extraordinary powers of communication, if its owner truly believes.

Meticulously, David draws the Star of David pattern on the computer screen. On each point he reconstructs the geometric facets and planes of each of the crystals he used in his original experiment. Then, ever so painstakingly, David constructs the complex jigsaw arrangement of atoms that comprises the Singer, the miniature replica of the great ship Moon Singer.

"Now," he directs himself, bracing for the impact, "I will carefully place the Singer at the apex of the triangle. Maybe, just maybe it will work."

But it doesn't. Absolutely nothing happens. Not a shimmer of light, not a quiver of movement. The illustration is dormant on the screen. The Wind Rose compass needle remains still.

"Rats! How can I do this? What do I need to make a connection?"

David begins entering programming codes, any numeric combination he can think of that relates to the geometric pattern that he created on the screen. As he does so, the screen blinks off, then on, then off again.

Panicked, David reboots the laptop hoping he hasn't lost his work. A blue screen appears, then a white screen, and then a vision that shocks David to his core.

Thirteen

"Holy cow - Holy cow!"

"Are you still using that juvenile expression, my dear David?" the holographic vision speaks to him. "Well, I suppose it's better than some of the words you young people use today."

David is speechless. His mouth hangs open in astonishment at the familiar sight of the capricious gypsy fortune teller.

"Come now, David. No words of welcome for an old friend? You do remember me, don't you?"

How well he remembers the delightful woman who cajoled him onto the Moon Singer the first time, to the Island of Darkness and his encounter with Ishtar and the beautiful Princess Saliana.

"Dorinda! My God. I can't believe it's you. And I can't believe I can hear you."

"Why are you surprised? You invoked me before and you heard me then. You still have the power."

"Yes, but I don't have the Singer. I didn't think I could ever hear again without it."

"It's just like riding a bike," she says, with that perpetual twinkle in her eyes. "Once you learn, you never forget how."

"I seem to have forgotten everything, Dorinda. My life is a shambles."

"This is no time for a pity party," she chides him, amiably. "You have more important things to do."

"Like what?"

"Like getting the Singer back, and finding the Rose Crystal."

"I almost had the Singer back the other day, but it washed out to sea before I could grab it. And the Rose Crystal was given away accidentally by my father. I don't know where to begin to look for it."

"Yes you do. Or you will. Once you go back to the Source, all things will be clear to you."

David chuckles. "Another of your cryptic clues. I think you have a file drawer full of them. Just what is the *Source*, Dorinda? I've been trying to figure that out."

"David, think. Didn't you come here today to summon the Moon Singer?"

"Well, yes."

"And you know the Moon Singer takes you on a journey to where you find solutions to your problems."

"But why do I always have to go somewhere else to solve my problems," David protests, "make some quantum leap into a fantasy dimension? My dad already thinks I'm crazy for trying to explain what I've been through, and Sally hardly believes anything I say anymore. I haven't accomplished much on my two trips."

"But you did, David. You accomplished a great deal. But you know that your journeys are not over. Your dissatisfaction demonstrates that you are still seeking answers to life's mysterious questions, as well as the solutions to mundane problems. Remember what you accomplished on the Island of Darkness and on Coronadus? These were monumental successes."

"But then I had a mission. When I sailed on the Moon Singer the first time it was to find Sally, to save her life. And when I went to Coronadus it was to communicate with my mother, to understand why she had to die. But this time I have no reason, no mission to accomplish."

"Your mission will reveal itself in a short time, David. Be available to it when it comes. I'll only say that, this time, it's more personal and more imperative than the others."

With that, the hologram of Dorinda disappears abruptly. In its place is the Star of David crystal diagram. A message box pops up asking, "Do you want to save this file?" David clicks on "yes" and the screen goes black.

The Wind Rose needle moves slowly a few degrees in a clockwise direction, then moves no more. David knows the Moon Singer is near, but he doesn't know why he wants her to come for him.

"More personal and more imperative than I can imagine," he repeats Dorinda's clue. "What could be more personal than finding Sally or seeing my mother again?"

David's stomach flutters with anxiety and anticipation knowing it is crucial that he find the Singer and the Rose Crystal for personal reasons; but he has yet to fully comprehend that by reuniting them with the Wind Rose - aligning the three sacred artifacts that have been coveted for centuries - phenomenal changes will occur in the world, in the present, and in the future.

He hopes Dorinda is right, that his newest mission will reveal itself very soon.

Fourteen

Dr. Ramirez works feverishly on his keyboards at the observatory lab, despite a pounding headache. The music he composes is lavish with dissonant chords in the Key of F#dim, setting into motion the masculine and feminine polarities of harmony, and the positive and negative forces of nature. Once he has a composition he feels achieves his objectives, he will load it into his computer and hook it up to the weather satellites.

First, he will impact Port Avalon, then jolt the USA, and then shock and terrorize the entire world.

He alone will know how to stop the catastrophes that will soon ravish the earth because he created them. He will be famous for his discovery. People around the globe will offer him large sums of money, all the riches in their national coffers, to reveal the secret codes to them that will stop the disasters. No one will ever know that he is the creator of the destructive harmonics; they will only know him as their savior.

Outside, the twilight sky begins to darken as afternoon becomes night. Needing a break, Ramirez engages the observatory's massive telescope, hoping to catch a glimpse of the shimmering, cloud-shaped light in the heavens that he had seen several times before. When at last the optical instrument brings the light into focus, Ramirez is ecstatic.

"It's got to be a lightship from some other planet! They hear the din, the chaos, and soon they'll swoop down on the earth and destroy all those who have committed crimes against music and humanity. But when they realize that I have the codes, they will allow me to live. Yes, they will need me. Together we will do great things and rule the galaxy!"

Ramirez' mad ranting is cut short by a shooting pain that surges through his head. He stumbles backward onto the swivel chair at his computer station, almost sliding off. The flashes of light and blurred vision are more severe than anything he has ever experienced before. He must get that CT scan that the doctor insists he have.

But as the pain subsides, the urgency Ramirez feels also lessens, and he returns to his primary task, his music. He ejects the disk from the keyboard's CD drive and loads it into his PC tower. With a few keystrokes Ramirez creates a hard drive file for the new composition and begins to implement his insane scheme.

Fifteen

Sally Nickerson is a junior at Port Avalon High School, a popular and active girl despite her infirmity. She aspires to become an instructor of therapeutic dance and is already working on a method to teach disabled people how to move gracefully and meaningfully to music. This evening her group of experimental students is meeting in the gymnasium. The floor here is spacious and allows freer movement for the class without the possibility of injury.

As the students manipulate their crutches, canes and wheelchairs in tempo to the lovely waltz, "Fascination," Sally is reminded of David's birthday celebration at Lighthouse Point Restaurant when she and her brother took to the dance floor. It was only her imagination, her wishful thinking, she knows, but that night she did throw away her crutches and dance free and light as a ballerina.

How Sally adores her brother. If it hadn't been for his fearless experiments with his crystals she would still be wheelchair bound. It was an accident that put her there, a horrible car crash that killed her mother, crippled Sally, and nearly destroyed her father with guilt. But it was also an "accident of fate" that allowed her to walk normally, if only for a short time. Or was it a mystical miracle?

Did she really relapse because Isaac inadvertently gave away the Rose Crystal pendant that healed her? Or was she herself just losing faith? Maybe it was her fault for not believing in David and his powers anymore. Maybe she brought the relapse on herself and caused the breech between her and her brother. Whatever the reason, Sally knows she must get on with her life and accept things as they are. She hopes David can do the same.

"Speaking of my brother," Sally says to herself, checking her watch, "he should be here to pick me up any minute. Okay everyone," she addresses the students, "class is over for tonight. Thank you for coming. See you next week."

The students, trailed by Sally, file out of the gymnasium, chattering excitedly about the progress they made that evening. But loud voices heard at the far end of the corridor startle everyone and they stop to look and listen.

It sounds at first like an argument, then a shouting match, and then turns into a real ruckus. One group of students, all natives of Port Avalon, harass a group of immigrant students who were attending an evening class. At first the transient boys and girls try to ignore the insults, but shoving begins, then pushing. Punches are thrown and an all-out brawl ensues.

Sally guides her dance class away from the fight and out the door to the main stairs. Terrified and angry parents who came to pick up their kids descend upon the school. Police cars, with sirens blaring and lights flashing, screech to a halt at the entrance. Armed officers race up the stairs to stop the fight.

Fortunately, all of Sally's students are safely escorted down the handicap ramp to their parents' or friends' cars. David pulls up and parks hastily in a slot nearby. He dashes up to the top of the stairs and to Sally's side.

"Holy cow, Sally. What's going on?"

"I don't know, David. This argument broke out and turned into a serious brawl. It's awful. There's never been anything like this at school, ever."

"Well, let's get you out of here and safely home."

Without warning, a deep and foreboding rumble is heard beneath the ground. Like waves rocking a boat, the ground shifts back and forth, moving the stairs in an undulating motion. The cement steps crack and separate. Sally screams as she loses her footing and tumbles down, hitting every one of the 15 rock hard crevices on her descent.

"Sally!" David yells while trying to maintain his own balance. He stumbles down a few steps but manages to keep upright. When the earth is finally still, David rushes down to Sally's motionless body. She has bruises and blood all over her face.

"Sally. Sally! Oh, no. Oh, God no! She can't be."

Sally moans and David gasps for air, relieved she is still alive. "Call 911," he yells. "Anybody! Please help! Please!"

* * *

"This is incomprehensible, just incomprehensible." Isaac rocks back and forth in the ER waiting room chair, tears of despair streaking down his face.

"Isaac," Janice comforts him, "we can be thankful that she's still alive."

"Alive? She's in a coma. She may never wake up, let alone walk again if she does wake up," Isaac sobs. "It's so unfair. After all she's been through."

David sits sullenly on the couch. Whatever his father feels, he feels it ten times more. He should have been able to hold onto her, should have protected her. *It should be me lying there, not Sally. Not my sister.*

Of course, he knows intellectually that he didn't cause the earth to tremor and the steps to shake apart so that Sally would fall. But an earthquake in Port Avalon is unheard of. The city is not on any fault line. So, what happened? Is it a warning, a harbinger of what will come if David keeps on dabbling in crystal power or esoteric computer pro-grams? Or is it happening because he *lost* the Singer and Rose Crystals, and cannot fathom how to summon their powers again?

David's heart is so heavy he doesn't think he can bear the weight of it. The pit of his stomach is a knot of regret, sadness, anger and nausea. There is nothing he can do at the hospital, so he leaves and walks out into the night, alone.

No one will miss me anyway. I'm to blame for Sally's condition. Everything that has happened since last summer is my fault. I know Dad blames me. He doesn't say it, but I can tell when he looks at me. He expected more from me, and I failed.

Sixteen

There is only one place David feels comfortable and safe, only one person he can trust and confide in. Picking up his stride, David makes his way to the Port Avalon Observatory, to his friend and mentor, Dr. Ramirez.

The lights in the lab are on, much to David's delight, and he is pleased to find the professor at his keyboard.

"Can I join you?" David asks as he sits down at his computer station. Ramirez is engrossed in his work and barely acknowledges him, but David is used to the professor's intense concentration on something he is passionate for.

David sets up his PC to network into Ramirez' keyboard, hoping to learn some new music. But when the sequences appear on David's screen, he is confused. Something isn't right. The harmonics are all over the place, the dissonant chords overwhelmingly prevalent. David can't hear the notes but he can tell there is something foreboding in what Ramirez is creating.

"Dr. Ramirez, what is that you're playing?" David sends an instant message, but Ramirez doesn't respond. He waves to get Ramirez's attention, but the professor shakes his head and gruffly orders, "Don't bother me now!"

Disappointed at being shut out, David sulks, while the bizarre vibrations and colors dance across his monitor. Unfamiliar numeric codes pop up on the screen and, along with them, a string of polyphonic chords and polyrhythms. The tempo changes are wild and rapid, from *allegro* to *presto* to *prestissimo*. The notations are so fast that David is overwhelmed trying to follow along.

Suddenly, David's PC tower shakes fiercely and almost topples to the floor. The room sways and shimmies.

"Dr. Ramirez! What's happening? Are you okay?"

David jumps up from his station to be by the professor's side. But Ramirez doesn't respond. He is fixated on his keyboards and the mad music he is playing.

"Stop!" David yells, and presses his hand firmly over the professor's. "What are you doing? Don't you feel the earthquake?"

With that, the shaking subsides and, as though it never happened, the professor looks up naively at David's confused and panicked expression.

"Feel what, David?"

"The earthquake! Didn't you feel the earthquake?"

"No, I didn't feel anything. Probably you felt me pounding the keyboards a bit too hard. Sorry. And actually, I'm kind of tired. I think I'll go now."

Ramirez rises up from his station and leaves the lab without as much as a farewell.

There's something crazy going on here. The worse Doc's music gets, the more the ecosystem goes crazy.

He loads a CD into the professor's PC tower to copy the music file.

I need time to sort this all out. I'll do it at home where I won't be bothering anyone, and they won't bother me.

Seventeen

Early the next morning, David decides to find some complete privacy to investigate the music file he copied. He carries his laptop to the beach, and checks to be sure the Wind Rose compass is secure in his pants pocket. He finds a makeshift wooden bench nestled in some rock formations and sits. He removes the Wind Rose from his pocket and sets it down on the bench beside him. *Just in case,* he muses about the Moon Singer. *You never know when she'll decide to appear.*

The laptop boots up and David opens Dr. Ramirez's music file that he downloaded from the CD. He studies the erratic tonal patterns, the strange rhythmic structure, trying to get a handle on the composition's theme, but it eludes and frustrates him. *I've never seen anything like this. I just can't decipher it. I'm actually glad I can't hear it.*

But David strongly suspects the professor's music has something to do with the bizarre weather and earth disturbances Port Avalon has been experiencing.

With no rhyme or reason, David begins to key in some chord symbols, flats and sharps, majors and minors, and diminished chords. When he keys in intervals - thirds, fifths, and sevenths, a formula flashes on the screen, one that David has seen before: 12 is 7 is 5 is 3. But its meaning still doesn't click in his brain.

David plays with the numbers, entering them in and out of order, but there are just so many combinations he can create. Getting a spark of inspiration, David decides to ask the computer exactly what the formula means.

"What is 12 is 7 is 5 is 3?" he types in.

"You know what it means, David." The instant reply startles him, but he replies back, "No, I don't know. What is 12 is 7 is 5 is 3?"

"Go back to the source, David. The choice is yours."

The choice is yours. That's what Dorinda told me the first time she and the Moon Singer appeared to me, when Sally vanished from her wheelchair. If I wanted to find her, I had to take the journey, unafraid, Captain the Moon Singer to her destination and to my destiny.

"But where?" David asks. "Where do I go back to? What is the Source? The Island of Darkness doesn't exist anymore, and neither does Coronadas. Besides, how do I go anywhere at all without the Moon Singer?"

A shadow across the sand alerts David that someone is standing beside him. Startled, he looks up to see Heather.

"Are you talking to yourself, David?" she signs, smiling amiably at him.

David shuts the laptop to shield the screen from her view, and stands to confront her. "How long have you been there?" he signs, agitated. "Are you spying on me?"

Taken aback by David's rudeness, Heather's expression transforms from genial to wounded. "No, David. I - I was just - taking a morning walk and saw you here. I only wanted to say hello to a friend. Why are you upset with me?"

"I'm not upset," David snaps. "I just want some privacy. I have a lot on my mind."

"What's wrong with you lately? You're always in a bad mood. Why don't you tell me what's going on. I want to help -"

"I don't want your help," David moves his fingers sharply. "There's nothing you can do anyway," he blurts out. "Sally's in a coma and it's all my fault! So just let me be."

Heather is shocked. This is the first she has heard about Sally. "In a coma? My God, David, what happened to her?"

"She fell down the stairs at the high school last night. I should have held on to her, but I didn't and she fell."

"I'm so sorry. But - she'll wake up soon - won't she? People do -"

"Soon? She may never wake up at all!"

Heather's eyes begin to well up, from both the news about Sally and David's anger towards her. "You can't blame yourself, David. It was an accident."

"There's no such thing as an accident. Not where me and my family are concerned. It's like we're cursed. The Nickerson curse, that's what it is." He picks up a sand pebble and tosses it angrily.

"David, I - I don't know what to say. I -"

"Don't say anything," David says, morosely. "Just go, before you fall victim to the curse, too."

Heather almost laughs, but the angst on David's face tells her he is not joking in the slightest.

"Go, I said! Leave me be!"

Stung to the core, Heather backs away from David, sobbing uncontrollably. Then she turns and runs off.

Feeling like a rat for hurting Heather, who has always been a friend to him, David plops down on the bench and holds his head in his hands. He is tired, confused, torn in five different directions. Nothing in his life is working. Nothing in Port Avalon is working. Everywhere he turns there is chaos, turmoil, anger, and devastation. He can't hear the actual sounds of it all, but he can feel the destructive force of it.

He longs to hear again, not the anger and conflict in his surroundings, but the angelic sound of Saliana's song. It was the first sound he had heard in years, and it carried him away to the most amazing adventure of his life on the most magnificent clipper ship one could imagine, to a place where he learned about love and courage and worlds beyond this one.

David opens his laptop and types in, "I want to go back. I'm ready to go back. To the Source, to where it all made sense."

At those words, at the instant his choice is made and his intention is set, David's laptop becomes a hierarchy of angels, with dancing beams of light emblazoning the sand.

"Holy cow!" he exclaims, thrilled by the sight. He picks up the Wind Rose. Its needle is spinning, round and round, from compass point to compass point. His heart fills with expectation and he is not disappointed. When the clipper ship appears before him, she is the same majestic, luminous vision on the water that he remembered. Sleek as satin, her awesome masts jutting proudly into the air, her silk sails bursting full into the skyline, the Moon Singer is the stuff of dreams, his dreams. And he is her Captain.

The great ship hovers a hundred yards out on the ocean, but his hand can reach out to touch her. She extends the gangplank inviting David aboard. He walks up the ramp, his feet never touching the sand, never skimming the water. The clipper raises the gangplank and sets out to sea, with David at the helm. As before, they sail together across the magnificent blue-green seascape, covering mile after mile of endless ocean in the blink of an eye, as David's hometown become a distant image.

Heather hides behind the rocks, shuddering at the sight before her. She cannot believe her eyes. It must be an illusion, no - a delusion. Or maybe she's asleep and dreaming. She can't be awake. Things like this don't happen except in dreams, or unless you're crazy and hallucinating. She has to tell someone, but who would believe her? There is no one else on this stretch of beach, no one to corroborate her story. And how could she tell, anyway? No words could describe what she has just seen.

Noticing David's laptop on the sand, she picks it up and the brilliant flashes of light on the screen mesmerize her.

What it is, she cannot fathom, but the dancing images of color are rhythmical and fascinating, and the sound - that glorious sound coming from the machine in her hand - is the most angelic music she has ever heard.

Eighteen

Unlike David's first voyage on the Moon Singer, which was fraught with raging storms and uncertainty, this trip is swift and direct, transcending time and space with record speed. This time there is no need to explore the gleaming white upper and lower decks of the great clipper ship to look for clues to his destination, or to marvel at the sight of the three towering masts of pure crystal encircled with solid gold rings. He knows that the Moon Singer was fashioned centuries ago by some very wise men who wanted to protect the power and knowledge they had accumulated, until the right person came along who would use the power for good and not evil.

David is ready for the voyage this time, eager to return to a place that enlightens and empowers him. Even though he has no clue what or who he'll be returning to, this alone – the leap into the unknown - invigorates him. He doesn't care if this foray is a dream, an illusion, or all in his mind for, as Ishtar once told him, "They are merely different levels of the same reality." *Although Dad thinks I'm completely out of touch with reality.*

Ishtar. The thought that he might meet up with the brilliant architect and engineer makes David even more eager to drop anchor. Will he see his old friend again, the man who gave him the courage to destroy the Glass Snake, rescue Saliana, and find his sister?

David's question is answered as the Moon Singer drifts toward land then halts a few hundred yards from shore.

A small boat, carrying David, is lowered to the water and David picks up the oars. The sky is azure and the sun a warm peach glow as David parks the skiff on the sugary white sand. He is greeted by a flock of sea birds that fly in formation toward a grove of trees, beckoning David to follow.

It is as he remembered, the mirrored pools of water, the strutting peacocks, the plush, emerald carpets of grass. It was once an Island of Darkness, overrun by evil and treachery, a place where people were enslaved and tortured into hopelessness, until David answered the call of Saliana's song and brought with him the impetus for their liberation.

David stands at the clearing and gazes at the towering sight on the summit of a hill. The Prism Palace is once again a shimmering vision before him, a dazzling display of every color of the light spectrum.

"Who lives there now?" David wonders. "Did Jaycina stay on the Island and become the kinder, gentler High Priestess she promised to be?"

"Well, my boy, come with me and you'll find out!"

David spins around and comes face to face with the owner of that resonant and familiar voice. "Ishtar! I can't believe it! I'm so happy to see you!"

"As am I to see you," the older man bellows jovially, pulling David into a bear hug of welcome.

"So this is what Dorinda meant by coming back to the Source. Returning to the Island of – but it's not the Island of Darkness anymore, is it?"

"Indeed not," Ishtar is happy to say. "Yes, it is technically still an island, of course, but now it is as I always intended, a magnificent city of technology and spirit combined, the cradle of all learning and enlightenment. I call it the Kingdom of Light."

"I can't wait to see everything, Ishtar. Please show me around."

"I will gladly be your tour guide, but first some good food and drink after your long voyage."

"As only Dorinda can make it?" David hopes. His mouth waters remembering her superior culinary skills.

"Even better than you remember," Ishtar says. He places his arm affectionately around David's shoulder and leads him down the main road to his house. "We have a lot to catch up on, you and I."

"I'll say. More than you can imagine."

Nineteen

David chows down on a fantastic meal prepared by Dorinda, as if it were his last meal... or the first good one he's had in a long time.

"I don't understand why I'm so hungry," David says, taking his third helping of Dorinda's famous stew.

"Inter-dimensional travel burns a lot of calories," Dorinda quips in her usual witty demeanor. She pats her flat stomach and declares, "I lose my middle every time I pay you a holographic visit." She finishes with a wink.

"Yes, then you get it back each time you find your way back to the kitchen and whip up one of your fattening new recipes," Ishtar teases her.

"You should talk," Dorinda jokes while serving Ishtar his favorite dessert. Theirs is a friendship that has stood the test of time, weathered every storm, and prevailed even in the darkest of Ishtar's moods when he thought he had lost everything in his life.

David laughs at both of them, happily accepting a plate of that luscious chocolate cake for himself.

The table setting is as splendid as Ishtar's home, a far cry from the underground cave he lived in when the Island was one of darkness and treachery.

Here on the reinvigorated island, David is happy. He feels a peacefulness that he doesn't feel in Port Avalon. Here, directions are clear and uncomplicated, the purpose is pure, the choices are distinct. At home, life is too complex, too many shades of gray, the line between right and wrong is blurred, even eradicated.

"I feel more like me here, like I have some connection to everything and everyone."

"Indeed you do," Ishtar tells him. "It's where you can be your true self, be with people who have loved and cherished you throughout many lifetimes. In fact, someone else is here that you will be happy to see."

"Saliana?" David looks around for her, hoping to see her lovely face, to hear her voice again. How he wished that he had told her the last time that he loved her, before he went home to Port Avalon. Maybe now he can rekindle their relationship and take it to a new level.

But instead of Saliana, the one who stands before him is the woman who has had the most important and enduring impact on his life.

"Saliana is on her way," the woman says, "But I wanted to greet you first." Bianca takes a seat at the dinner table next to David.

Bianca is there! In the Kingdom of Light. In Ishtar's house, at his table. David is speechless and emotional.

"Mom." he whispers.

Bianca puts a finger to her lips, indicating that David not say this aloud. Then she kisses him gently on his cheek.

"You never knew this," Ishtar says, "but Bianca is my wife. Saliana's mother."

David is dumbfounded. "Your wife? Saliana's – "

The fact that Bianca is Saliana's mother has profound implications for David. He looked upon this woman as a mother figure – his own mother, reincarnate – but that would make him Saliana's – brother? So much for things being simpler here than at home.

Something even more astonishing occurs to David. "But why weren't you all together on the Island? Why was Bianca on Coronadus?"

"You recall what was happening on the Island before you came," Ishtar says.

"You mean Jaycina and her plan to take control of everything and everyone?"

Ishtar nods. "It wasn't the Island of Darkness then. It was just our island, one I envisioned would become a mecca of learning and healing and advanced technology. Jaycina desperately wanted to own my plans, my designs, and all the precious energy resources. I couldn't let that happen, so my family and I had to escape. We took only our most essential belongings, then we burned down our house. I let Jaycina believe that everything she coveted was in it."

"We almost got completely away," Bianca interjects, "but there was an unexpected earthquake. Deep crevices in the earth split in a bizarre pattern right under our feet. I was caught on one side, Ishtar and Dorinda were on the other side. We were completely separated from one another."

"But what about Saliana? What happened to her?"

"I had stumbled on the path and almost fell through a hole in the ground," Saliana explains, now coming forth to join the trio and accepting a cup of tea from Dorinda.

She is even more beautiful than I remembered, David thinks. Her hair is still a cascade of golden curls, her eyes clear and penetrating, her voice a lilting warmth. His heart quivers at the sight of her, but his stomach turns over at the revelation that they may be related somehow.

"I held onto a tree root and screamed for Mother or Father to help me," Saliana continues her story, "but they couldn't reach me. After the earth stopped shaking, we were all alive but completely apart. There was no way either of them could get to me. Then I heard *them*."

"Who?"

"Jaycina's sentries. They wanted all of us, but I was the only one within their grasp. They rescued me only to imprison me in the Palace Tower. You know the rest."

"How could I forget," David says, as all the pictures of those days on the Island of Darkness flash across his mind like a movie. "And I know that Ishtar and Dorinda took refuge in a secluded cave. But, Bianca, how did you get from the Island to Coronadus?"

"I'm not really certain," Bianca replies. "I wanted so much to be with my husband and my daughter, but I couldn't transcend that split. I even tried to transport myself to their side using the Wind Rose - "

"The Wind Rose!" David exclaims. "You had it?"

"Yes, David. It was the Wind Rose that took me to Coronadus, to another point in time. But I lost it somewhere along the way. It was as though there was an interruption in the sequence of energy systems."

"But it was there, in the shop in Coronadus," David reminds her. "I found it by – *not* by accident, right?"

"Yes. Not by accident. When you chose the Wind Rose for your souvenir it was destiny, and I knew that through our meeting I would be reunited with my family."

Other: In the past and present, in the heavens and on earth, in time and space... and in his mother's heart...

David tries to absorb all of this new information, feeling some of it resonate with familiarity, but it hurts his brain. Bianca had once told him that some things are beyond our current level of understanding. We need more data, more proof, more experience before we can bring it all into a cohesive awareness. So far, the ability to completely understand his relationship to these three people is beyond him. The mystical experiences, his encounters with people, places and things from other times, other dimensions are things he just can't quite wrap his mind around. The metaphysical aspect, the karmic connections, the intertwining of lives and destinies are still too complex to grasp. It was all a chain reaction – his experiments with the Singer, the appearance of the Moon Singer, his arrival on the Island.

Other: The mystery is infinitely deep and the desire for answers will open a Pandora's Box of trouble as well as a treasure chest of good fortune...

Suddenly, David remembers something. Had he known what he was doing when he invoked the power of the Star of David that first time, he would have sailed the Moon Singer into a Kingdom of Light instead of an Island of Darkness. All the troubles, misery and suffering that plagued Ishtar's family and the Islanders would never have happened.

"The earthquake," David chastises himself, "happened when I used the Star of David to ignite the Singer. I was the reason. My foolish experiment interrupted your lives."

"Yes," Ishtar concedes. "That's how you got to the Island. But remember what else I told you, that we merely had an inter-dimensional collision causing all of our destinies to become intertwined. It was accidental on your part, but also meant to be. Your first karmic lesson was with Saliana and I. In rescuing us, you helped rescue your own family from their dilemmas."

Other: ... the fairy tale daydreams have served their purpose...

"But I wasn't finished."

"That's right, David," Bianca says. "Your next karmic lesson was your encounter with me on Coronadus."

Other:... his mother's heart is now wide open to embrace and guide his path to discovery...

"To resolve my conflicted feelings about my mother, my anger over her dying."

"Yes. And so that I would be able to return to my family, and here to my home."

"And still I'm not finished," David says with exasperation. "Why am I here now?"

Ishtar laughs heartily. "Well, you brought yourself here this time, willingly. So, you tell us."

David smiles back, slightly embarrassed. "I'm not sure. I wanted to escape the chaos happening at home. As usual."

Other:... he is ready to delve into more complex questions and deal with answers that may shock and surprise him...

"Well, let's explore the Island," Ishtar invites him, "and perhaps you will find the answer."

Twenty

Standing majestically on the highest hill of the Island, is the Prism Palace, the shimmering vision he remembers. It appears to be a crystal of monolithic proportions, deceptively transparent, with near-blinding refractions of light that obscure its interior from view. Angular and defined, a geometric puzzle with smooth and seamless interlocking pieces, the palace is comprised of a tetragon on the left, a trigonal on the right, and a hexagonal center that towers over all.

He is compelled to run to its threshold, just as he did that first time, to let the Celestial rainbows of color wash over him, embrace him, consume him. But David also recalls that the Palace interior was a labyrinth of peril from which he had to rescue Saliana who was cruelly imprisoned in the Tower, and escape the clutches of the evil Jaycina.

Jaycina, David learns, no longer inhabits the Prism Palace as High Priestess. With her metamorphosis from malevolent temptress into a benevolent matriarch, Jaycina's mission was finished and she moved on to another time and place. David believes that Jaycina's spirit embodies Janice Cole who, herself, had a transformation from being an accommodating subordinate to that rat Nathan Fischbacher, to the courageous and astute woman who beat Nathan at his own game and saved Cole Shipping.

Ishtar and David tour the miraculous new city, one that Ishtar had envisioned, and then finally manifested. The architecture of every structure that Ishtar designed and built is spectacular, and David marvels at the temples of Science and Nature, Medicine and Healing, and Humanistic Understanding. But his favorite is the Temple of Music and Miracles, once the ominous Prism Palace. It is where Saliana studies with the Temple's music master, Rami.

"This is amazing," David remarks. "Here you have an entire temple devoted to music and yet in Coronadus where Rami lived there was no music at all let alone a Temple for it."

"You are correct," Ishtar concurs. "I'm sure if you think about it for a moment, you can figure out why."

"Me? Figure it out? Uh - well, can you give me a hint?"

"All right," Ishtar agrees. "You remember how enthralled you were with Saliana's song -"

"Yes, that beautiful song about the Moon Singer. It was the first sound I had heard since before I went deaf. It was as though an angel was calling me and I followed it to the Island."

"Well, it was Rami who programmed Saliana's song with secret musical codes that correlate to the codes in the Rose Crystal Pendant. This is why her music has miraculous healing power and why your sister was able to rise out of her wheelchair and walk."

"Because Saliana gave me the Rose Crystal to bring home for Sally," David concludes. "And... oh, no... because I had the Rose Crystal, there could be no Temple of Music here."

David is distraught, to think that, again, he was the cause of Ishtar's loss. First his experiments with crystals caused an earthquake that separated Ishtar and his wife, and then his taking the Rose Crystal home with him also meant he was taking away all music from Coronadus.

"But now we have it back again," Ishtar tells him soothingly.

"But how?" David asks, confused. "The Rose Crystal is missing. My father accidentally gave it away."

"Your father didn't really give it away, David. I took it back." Again, Saliana appears as if from nowhere.

David turns sharply at the sound of her voice. "You did? Why, Saliana? Why would you do that to Sally?"

Twenty-one

"The Rose Crystal was created to heal and to sustain life through its music, but right now it is troubled," Saliana explains, now joining David and Ishtar on their walkabout. "It is picking up damaging vibrations in the atmosphere of your Port Avalon, and that's what interfered with Sally's recovery. I couldn't take the chance that the codes would be broken or discovered by someone who had ill motives."

"What do you mean?"

"There are things happening in your home town that are disruptive - the fighting, the prejudice, the environmental problems, the erratic weather changes, the fear of an Apocalypse. They all point to a breakdown in Universal Law, especially the laws of music."

"Amazing! That's just what Dr. Ramirez says," David tells her.

"He's right," Saliana agrees. "But he is not being completely truthful with you."

"Why? Why would he lie to me?"

Rami, also appearing from no discernible place interjects, "I suspect that your Dr. Ramirez is creating the destructive musical vibrations."

David refuses to believe it. The professor has been acting strange lately, and that new composition that David downloaded from Dr. Ramirez's keyboard is wildly out of control. But his idol and mentor could not possibly create havoc in the world with the music he so loves. It must be a mistake.

"Maybe he is doing it accidentally," David suggests, "I mean there are only so many combinations of notes."

"Actually, musical variety is virtually infinite," Rami corrects him. "There are strings, winds and percussion instruments all making their own unique sounds with the same notes. A middle C on a piano sounds very different from middle C on a violin. Then you have the unique tenor of an electronic synthesizer. Add to this the fact that more than one note and more than one instrument can be played at the same time, and qualities like pitch, timbre, loudness and duration all enter into the equation."

"I know it's a real long shot, but considering the law of averages, mathematically speaking, after all these years of creating music, couldn't someone just stumble upon the combination and not know it?"

"It's possible. Remotely possible," Rami concedes. "But if they did it unconsciously they would also unconsciously reject the patterns."

"I don't understand."

"It all comes down to intent," Saliana explains. "When people create music, they have the intention of evoking a response, usually a pleasant or favorable one."

"Like romance or happy memories," David submits. "But what about anger or power or control?"

"People *use* music to do this, but they don't usually *create* it with this intention."

"But Hitler used the music Wagner created to stir up the German masses to Nazism," David corrects Saliana.

"Yes, but Wagner didn't create his music for this perverted purpose," Rami corrects David. "His intention was to shock and provoke, yes, but to lift people up to a different way of thinking, to self-empowerment not self-destruction. I think whoever is writing the dissonant music in Port Avalon knows it can destroy, because that is his conscious intent."

"But why do you think it's Dr. Ramirez? What's his motive?"

"Well, that's the question, isn't it?" Rami suggests. "What *is* his motive?"

"Whatever it is, we've got to stop him," David says, emphatically. "I'll just go tell him he has to stop, that he's hurting people and could destroy the entire town."

"I doubt he will be stopped that easily. We need to find out why he has turned his passion into a malevolent obsession. And when we do, his impulses will have to be reversed."

"Well, if we tell the authorities and he goes to jail, that will stop him!"

"No, no. We can't make it public," Rami warns. "If we do, there are others who would go to any lengths to have these codes, to hold the entire world hostage. No. No one must know what is happening."

Twenty-two

"Rami, you went to extraordinary lengths to protect the Singer," Ishtar says later, when the two of them meet alone, "nearly drowning to keep it safe. But now it must be returned to David. He needs it. Why are you so hesitant?"

When Coronadus was destroyed by Bianca, in an effort to save the people she loved, Rami was washed out to sea in the tidal wave. Although David tried to rescue him, he couldn't, and Rami and the Singer disappeared beneath the turbulent water. Before he sank to the depths of the ocean, Rami promised David he would protect the sacred crystal just as David had to protect the Wind Rose.

But when David asked Rami where the Singer was and if he could have it back, Rami was evasive and told David that he will give it to him when the time is right.

"I want him to use it right this time, when he returns home with it," Rami insists to Ishtar. "He must realize the importance and the ramifications of his ownership of all three artifacts, especially the Singer."

"I believe David knows fully its importance," Ishtar defends David.

"But he must understand why he was given the power to sail the Moon Singer. He can't just continue to play around with crystals and grid patterns and accidentally fall into a solution," Rami protests.

"Well, it was no accident this time. He deliberately set out to conjure up the Moon Singer and come back here, not even knowing what his mission is."

"Yes, he had the intent," Rami counters, "but it was still just luck that he entered the proper codes into his computer, even if they were in random sequence."

"On a subconscious level he knows them, or else how could he come up with them?" Ishtar is getting a bit perturbed at Rami's intransigence.

"He must *consciously* know," Rami says, more emphatic than ever. "Until he comes to a full realization, it's all luck and his karmic lessons will not come full circle." "Then, show him his soul code," Ishtar demands. "Part of his not knowing is your insistence he discover all for himself. It wouldn't hurt you to nudge things in his direction a bit. There is a lot at stake here."

"I don't know," Rami hedges. "He may not be ready. He's just a boy."

"He is an extraordinary boy. He is ready," Ishtar insists. "And he *will* get it."

"But will the people of Port Avalon get it?"

Twenty-three

As David and Saliana walk alone together in the magnificent gardens, catching up on old times and new, he talks about his hearing.

"There is an operation that can make me hear again back home. It's called a cochlear implant."

"Is this what you want?" Saliana asks.

"I don't know. I love being here where I can hear everything. I still don't understand it. When I was here before, I needed the Singer to help me hear, but now I don't have it and I can hear perfectly."

"When it was the Island of Darkness, there was so much chaos and treachery – interference in the air waves, Father likes to say – that you needed an instrument like the Singer to help you hone in on the important sounds. But now, in the Kingdom of Light, everything is harmonious, and you can hear with clarity without the crystal."

"If it works here, why can't it work at home?"

"That is your choice, David. So far, you have chosen to remain deaf at home."

"Bianca once said that to me. I chose to be deaf. I questioned it then, but now I'm beginning to understand karmic choices and their consequences. My deafness was a way for me to be closer to my mother, even after her death, so I could understand why she chose to die."

"And do you understand?"

"Well, sort of. Bianca made me see that it was Mom's way of atoning for the spiritual mistake of convincing her sister to join the war protest where she was killed."

"That's pretty heavy Karma." Saliana touches David's arm compassionately, and he places his hand over hers.

"It sure is. You know, I try to tell my Dad about all this and he thinks I'm being irrational, and maybe a bit crazy. He even brought a shrink home to talk to me about all of it. He especially can't understand why I refuse any more treatment or surgery to help me hear again."

"And you think he feels you are imperfect," Saliana says, completing his thoughts.

"Yes! How did you know?"

"Perhaps it's because I sense that you yourself feel imperfect, which could be part of the reason you keep trying to escape from home, to a magical place where you can hear the things you wish to hear."

"Bianca said pretty much the same thing." Changing the subject, he looks into Sally's clear blue eyes. "You remind me so much of my sister," David says, feeling tenderness in his heart for both girls, but in totally different ways. "Tell me, did Sally choose to be crippled after the car crash?"

"I don't think so, David. I think it just happened so fast she didn't have time to choose the outcome."

"Then if the Rose Crystal didn't cure her, what will?"

Saliana opens the collar of her dress to reveal the Rose Crystal Pendant, and removes it from her neck and places it in David's hand.

"I told you why it didn't work before, but I think things will be different this time. When I took it back, I reprogrammed the crystal with your Soul Code, David. It is actually you, your heart, body and soul that will create the miracle for Sally to wake up from her coma and walk again. This time for good."

"Me? I don't understand?"

"You will. Rami will explain it to you. He will tell you that there is one very important task you must perform before giving Sally the

Rose Crystal pendant. The decision that you make will have profound implications on your own future."

"What do I have to do?"

"As I said, Rami will explain it all. And then you will choose your destiny."

"This is all very confusing. I know, don't say it," he smiles and holds up his hand to stop her reply. "It will all be clear to me in time."

"I do believe you're getting it." Saliana nods her approval, and smiles a smile that lights up the already glowing place in David's heart.

"Tell me one thing, though, Saliana. Does my destiny – does it include you at all. I mean, if I stay here, would there be a chance for us?"

Saliana giggles. "You mean as brother and sister?"

"Oh, boy. I keep forgetting. Or just want to forget. But if it's true, then we can't be anything but friends."

"Well, it's sort of true," she says. "Our lives have touched – yours, mine, Ishtar's, Bianca's, Dorinda's – many times over. We have all at one time or another been brother and sister, husband and wife, father and mother and child. But you and I, now, are not related. I am but a symbol of your sister Sally, because you so desperately wanted to find her when she disappeared, and you saw in me the vehicle to save her."

David is relieved to say the least. He will let the reincarnation stuff alone right now. In this very moment, all he wants to do is touch Saliana's face gently, and kiss her lips sweetly. "I have wanted to tell you for so long, that I love you, Saliana."

"And I love you, David. But your destiny is not here with me. There is a great love waiting for you back home. It's right under your nose, but you don't see it."

"Home. As much as I want to go home, I do want to stay here a while longer, with you," David says, holding her close.

Saliana responds by placing her cheek against his. "For the moment, we can be together and create more wonderful memories. At least, until the Moon Singer beckons and you must leave."

"Why does the Singer conjure up the Moon Singer – a clipper ship?" David asks, changing the subject. "Why not a jet plane or space capsule in this day and age?"

"It's what your family is about," Saliana tells him, "your heritage. Sailing the Moon Singer has a tranquility about it, a peacefulness. You could not hear the things you needed to hear if jet engines were roaring all around you."

"I never thought of it that way."

Twenty-four

But all is not as harmonious in the Kingdom of Light as it should be. Surprising and erratic changes in the weather occur, small earth tremors are felt, and a brief but shocking eclipse of the sun bodes ill for the city. This latter incident truly stirs fear in the hearts of everyone. It's a reminder of how they lived in a constant state of night when the treacherous Glass Snake and the High Priestess Jaycina ruled the Island of Darkness with brutality and greed, usurping all the energy and light on the Island for their own benefit.

Even David's Wind Rose compass goes haywire, and the Moon Singer sways and rocks uneasily on a perilous sea.

"It's your Dr. Ramirez," Rami proclaims. "He has penetrated the earth's atmosphere with his irresponsible and dangerous music, and now threatens every dimension in the universe. He must be stopped!"

"But how, Rami? What can we do?"

"I will give you the tools to stop him."

"Me? Oh, no. Not me. I have a tendency to mess things up. This is too important."

"Music is a powerful demonstration of man's ability to connect with the Divine Creator," Rami tells him. "It is a symbol of what you, yourself, are made of, what you are capable of. Once you tap into the Triune Power of universal music you will touch the face of God and put an end to Ramirez's unholy scheme."

"Triune Power? I never heard of it," David replies, becoming anxious and feeling inept. "How can I tap into something I don't know anything about?"

"You do know, David."At least to a limited degree now. You've heard of the Trinity, in religious teachings."

"You mean like Father, Son and Holy Ghost? That Trinity?"

"Yes, exactly. But it's grander than even that. Think of the number 3. Everything that you are, have done, will do, is comprised of the number 3. You've acquired three sacred relics: the Singer, the Rose Crystal, and now the Wind Rose. Separately they are miracles unto themselves: the Singer with its all-encompassing knowledge, the Rose Crystal with its healing energies, and the Wind Rose, with both its power to destroy as well as to transcend reality. Synergistically, they are Divine in the truest meaning of the word: the represent the Power of One."

"But I don't have them all!" David protests. "And even if I did, what do I do with them? And how will I know what I'm doing?"

...you have merely scratched the surface of your capacity to recognize what you can become...

"What did you say?" David asks Rami.

"I said, you must discover that yourself," Rami insists. "I will now give you the tools. You must learn to use them as no one else can. You've chosen this path, David. You've invited these experiences into your life for reasons that only you can know, truly know."

Rami places the Singer into David's hand.

"You had it all along! You didn't lose it in the sea!"

"No," Rami admits. "I didn't lose it. I saved it for you, to give it to you when the time was right. Now here is what you must do..."

* * *

David now has the sacred Singer crystal, the Rose Crystal Pendant, and the Wind Rose compass - the three most important elements he needs to fulfill the mission Rami has designated for him.

The first thing David wants to do is return to the hospital, to place the Rose Crystal around Sally's neck, to let the pendant work its magic of healing on her.

She'll wake up, I just know it, he believes. *She'll be whole and healthy and all this will be just a bad dream. But first…*

Rami told David it would be the last of his three missions, but he was cryptic with his instructions. He left a good bit of it up to David's intuition, which in David's mind was a fool's errand. Despite all of his best efforts, everything that has happened to him has been either an accident - or not; preordained - or by choice; wishful thinking or divine intervention.

What is this other thing I must do before I can help Sally? Will I even recognize it when I see it? Oh, God, how can I decide what to do? He had to believe that this time it would be different.

Unbeknownst to David, Bianca returns with him as his special guardian. It is to be her last mission as well.

Twenty-five

David did not want to leave the Island now, any more than he had wanted to leave the first time. Nor had he wanted to leave Coronadus and Bianca - his mother. He came home with mixed feelings, unwilling to let go of the people he had come to know and love, and had no idea if he would ever see again.

Yet, he wanted to return home, for he knew he was bringing something special back with him, some special knowledge or tools that would help change their circumstances for the better. But more than just being able to help resolve the routine, but urgent, issues of his dad's unemployment or the town's financial woes as he had in the past, there was something more. There was something deep inside him testing his courage and his devotion.

That "something" floated around in his brain, in voices that came to him in the night or in daydreams, or popping up involuntarily during conversations with Ishtar, Saliana or Bianca. That "something" was about purpose, about destiny, about a deep desire to give of himself in ways he never imagined.

Other: To save a life that means more to him than his own...

* * *

Back in Port Avalon, people start seeing visions in the night sky, the visions once only witnessed by observatory astronomers with powerful telescopes. An opaque elliptical image with a glimmering outline soars across the evening sky, then dissipates. A translucent obelisk-shaped form moves out of the clouds, illuminating the starless Port Avalon night. A shimmering, cumulous cloud-shaped light glides across a part of the heavens. Each of the images is seen at different times and different places by different people.

After the sightings, other worrisome problems occur. People become more fanatical in their beliefs. Some think they see UFO's, others think the visions are fallen angels or a sign of the Apocalypse. The entire town is on edge as never before. And a mass hysteria begins to rumble beneath the surface of the otherwise tranquil coastal town.

Isaac hurries David along so they won't be late for the discussion at the Port Avalon town hall. Janice has checked on Dorothy, and feels the nurse has everything under control, but has her beeper on just in case. And the status report on Sally is that she is comfortable but there is no change in her condition. She still sleeps her dreamless sleep.

So, the three of them decide they need some diversion for the evening, especially such an important event.

"I don't know why I should go to this thing," David complains. "Just more psychobabble, especially if Hilyer is there."

David's "trip" to the Kingdom of Light never registered with Isaac and Janice. They never knew he was gone, as though those moments were frozen in time. It was as though they, themselves, were on some other plane of existence that suppressed their memory of his absence.

And on his return, though he hoped through some magic it would be better, David's relationship with his father has not improved. He doesn't dare mention this latest foray to a world beyond. His father would have him committed for sure.

"There are things going on in Port Avalon that are inexplicable and unacceptable," Isaac says. "I hear that this guest speaker is really wonderful. I can't remember her name, but Dr. Hilyer said it promises to be a great discussion with her on the panel. Maybe she can provide some solutions."

The Town Hall is packed. David, Isaac and Janice take their seats in a side box that will allow David to see the sign language interpreter. The moderator introduces Dr. Hilyer who takes his seat on the dais. David's head is bowed in indifference and he does not see the woman who is introduced next as, "Dr. Bianca Creighton, a renowned motivational speaker on the lecture circuit."

"Tonight," the moderator promises, "science, psychology and spirituality will intertwine in an evocative and provocative session."

"Wow, look at her," Isaac says, poking David's arm. "Isn't she stunning?"

David looks up to see a beautiful, statuesque woman, whose head is wrapped in a colorful, silken turban, one all too familiar to him. His mouth drops open as Bianca, *his* Bianca, takes her seat.

"A real looker, isn't she," Isaac whispers to Janice. Janice gives Isaac a sidelong glance of disapproval. Or is that jealousy in her eyes?

"There is no Armageddon, a one-time conflict defining all times, all ages," Dr. Hilyer says in response to the moderator's question. "The battle of good and evil is eternal, constant, day to day. The concept of the final battle is metaphorical, an inner fight for each of us."

"The things going on in the world," Bianca Creighton counters, "are not just metaphysical illusions. We can't just meditate them away. They are real manifestations of man's great potential for wickedness."

"I agree," Hilyer says. "We have to respond in a real way. Obviously the consciousness-raising of the past 30 years or so hasn't made a dent. Civilization is just as brutal and erratic as ever. We need more education, more psychological help for people who are violent, disenfranchised, and delusional."

"We pour millions – billions – of dollars into social programs, Dr. Hilyer," Bianca differs forcefully, "and people are more dysfunctional and violent than ever. There is no accountability. We live in an age where medical science has outpaced morality, where technology is light years ahead of the law, and where ethics is an anachronism. We have all the education and knowledge we need, but we are not using it wisely."

"Can you elaborate on that, Dr. Creighton?" the moderator asks, giving her more time.

"People, especially men, choose violence as a solution to everything..."

Boy, does this sound familiar, David muses. *That's what Bianca said on Coronadus before my disaster of a debate in front of the War Council.*

"Hold on," Dr. Hilyer interrupts, "are you saying that only men are violent?"

"Women don't wage war, Dr. Hilyer. Men do."

"More and more women are getting involved in foreign affairs and making military decisions," Hilyer rebuts Bianca's remarks, "and today, young girls are becoming aggressive, committing violent acts."

"Because they live in a man's world. And because there isn't enough money in peace these days. We have the science to neutralize radiation at the source. It would save lives. But a cleaner bomb would also be easier to use. It would eliminate the threat of annihilation, but normal people don't make these decisions. Everything is controlled by the oil conglomerates, the banking cartels, the munitions manufacturers."

"Well, we're getting off track here," the moderator reminds them. "We are talking about the Millennium phenomenon, the behavioral changes that occur when a moment in time has historic implications on people's spiritual beliefs, their fears and their behavior."

"Excess, fear, self-indulgence, intolerance – these are not just qualities of the 'millennium' generations. Every civilization has demonstrated them for centuries. But no civilization before this one has had the means at their fingertips to transcend the temptations of self-aggrandizement, of brutality, of destruction of the environment. And yet, we don't transcend. Instead, we repeat our destructive habits over and over again. If we pay heed to this new Millennium as a catalyst for change, then let's hope we use it wisely."

"Well, I'm not as disillusioned with the human race as you are, Dr. Creighton," Hilyer interjects while he has the chance. "When a catastrophe happens, people come together to help their neighbors and to find solutions."

"Yes, yes, this is true." Bianca acquiesces. "But in time they forget to be compassionate and unified, and resume their old ways. Then, another catastrophe occurs to bring people together again, and the cycle goes on. As an analogy, people sleep, then they wake up, then sleep again. Over and over. How many times must we do this until we *Get it?*"

...I have so grown tired of the journeys, the repetitious teaching of the same lesson over and over again...

The applause is deafening. The message is clear and tough. Tonight, it seems, the audience does Get it. How long will they keep it?

After the debate, Isaac invites Dr. Creighton to dinner. David keeps his counsel and says nothing to disclose that he and Bianca know each other, *more* than know each other, that they have a bond that transcends time and space, past and present. Bianca herself maintains a cordial but aloof recognition of David as only a charming boy who is Isaac's son.

Throughout the evening, Janice is strangely perturbed. This is not like her. She is acting differently, not the gracious woman she usually is with guests.

Later, when they are alone, Janice and Isaac have a fight, their first real disagreement.

"I don't understand why you are blowing this so out of proportion, Jan," Isaac chastises her.

"Don't talk to me like that, Isaac. I'm not a child. That's how Nathan used to talk to me, patronizing and paternalistic."

"Believe me, I know that. And Nathan certainly discovered you were more than a match for him. But I've never seen you like this. Pouty and sullen. It's not like you at all."

"No, it's not," Janice agrees, and feels an anxious chill up and down her spine. "And I hate it in myself! I just have this sense of foreboding around Dr. Creighton. I can't explain it, but I feel I'm losing you to her."

"Losing me? But we just met today. That's not even possible, let alone feasible."

"Maybe you'd better take me home, Isaac. No, on second thought I'm going home on my own. I'll call a taxi."

"Don't do this. You're being...unreasonable, Jan. This is so unlike you."

"Perhaps...we should call of our engagement...for now. Until Dr. Creighton leaves, or I can sort out my feelings."

"What!" Isaac is shocked. "No...Jan...wait. Don't go!"

Janice rushes off and Isaac is left with bewilderment.

"Now what the heck was that all about," Isaac wonders aloud, exasperated and confused. He looks at David beseechingly, and pleads "What did I do?"

Twenty-six

But soon more pressing incidents occur than a tiff between Janice and Isaac. Heavy storms hit Port Avalon, causing mudslides and more cliff erosion by the beach. The Nickerson family cemetery and especially David's mother's grave are in danger of being washed away. And an especially heavy blow to Isaac and Cole Shipping occurs when the Miracle Ship is badly damaged by flying debris and her maiden voyage has to be postponed.

But as swiftly and violently as the storm came, it subsides, and an eerie calm looms over the town.

Taking a walk along the beach, now marred by piles of seaweed and sea trash, where he had last summoned the Moon Singer, David looks around anxiously for his laptop. It's not on the bench where he left it and he fears it was washed out to sea, or worse yet, stolen by someone who might discover what was on the computer.

"Is this what you're looking for?" Heather says, holding the laptop toward David.

Trying to be casual while his stomach pulsates fearfully, David asks, "Where did you find it? I guess I must have left it somewhere. I'm getting forgetful." He takes the laptop from Heather and sits on the bench.

"You know exactly where you left it, David," Heather says apprehensively. "You left it here, that day I saw you and we argued. You told me to go away and leave you alone."

"I'm really sorry," David signs, with truly heartfelt expression. "I had no right to say those things to you. I hope you'll forgive me."

"Of course, I forgive you," Heather signs back. "I just don't understand you. In fact, after what I saw – I – I'm kind of afraid of you."

"What you saw? I don't know what you mean," he says evasively.

Heather stands in front of him. "I saw the lights, the brilliance from your computer. I saw the *ship*, and you, walking – good grief, I'm crazy! – walking on water!"

David wants to laugh at Heather's description, but he realizes that's what it would look like to someone else.

"And then you disappeared on this ship. Or maybe there wasn't a ship. Maybe you just disappeared. David, I don't even know if what I saw was real!"

"Maybe it's better you don't know," he tells her. "Just tell yourself it was a mirage or something."

"A mirage is what you see in the desert when you're dying of thirst. That's not what I saw."

"Sorry, I didn't mean to be patronizing. It's just too hard to explain. I can't do it right now. All I ask is that you keep this to yourself for now. Okay? No one else can know what you saw."

Heather throws back her head and laughs at the irony. "Don't worry. No one would believe me anyway." She sits down on the bench next to David. "And considering everything that's happening now in town, they might want to burn me at the stake."

Twenty-seven

Dr. Ramirez is in the lab, playing his keyboards and manically manipulating the weather systems. While he plays, he watches several TV monitors broadcasting weather reports from around the world.

David confronts him, and begs him to stop, but Ramirez refuses and becomes physical, pushing David against the wall, threatening to hold him hostage to keep him from telling anyone.

"I promise I won't tell anyone," David says, remembering Rami's warning not to. "But can't you at least tell me why you are doing this?" David pleads with him.

Ramirez gets hold of himself and releases David from his grip. "Because I'm fed up with noise blocking out every natural sound in the environment. Disgusted with the direction music has taken, away from its true meaning since the beginning of time. It's an insult to all the artists who have made so many sacrifices to leave the world a timeless musical legacy."

"You could do that, leave a legacy of great music, Dr. Ramirez," David suggests, hoping to get through to him. "Don't stoop to the level of the very people you despise."

Ramirez suddenly grabs his head and cries out in pain. He staggers away from his keyboards and almost falls to the floor, but David grabs him and sits him down.

"What's wrong? Are you hurt? Let me call an ambulance."

"No! No. It's just a headache. I have to finish my work."

"You are finished, at least for the night, professor. You've done enough damage."

"I might be finished for good, David. I think I'm dying."

David is almost relieved to hear what might be a plausible, and less villainous, reason for his friend's behavior. "Why? Are you sick? What is it?"

"I don't know. But I see things, in the telescope. Sometimes I think I see UFO's and sometimes I think I see angels. Whatever they are, they're coming to get me. I have something they want, David. I have the musical formulas that create and destroy life."

David is even more puzzled than before. Maybe the man is sick, or demented. It wouldn't excuse his behavior but it would at least explain it.

"When do you see these – these lights, Professor?"

"I saw them tonight. Before you came. Go ahead, look for yourself. If you see them, maybe I'm not dying. Or maybe we all are."

David powers up the telescope and studies the sky. At first he doesn't see anything out of the ordinary. He adjusts the lens to get a panoramic view, then he sees it, the image that Ramirez refers to. David knows exactly what it is, but he can't tell the professor or anyone else. Not yet.

"I think I see it, Dr. Ramirez." David turns away from the telescope to talk to his friend, hoping to pacify him. "It's not a UFO. It kind of looks like the vision some other people are describing. I'm sure there's a logical explanation. But, you know, "David says, feeling real concern for the man, "you really should see a doctor about your headaches. They could really be serious."

"I'm better now. Just eye strain," Ramirez says, straightening himself up and taking a refreshing breath. "Well, back to work. It's getting late, David. You'd better get on home."

With that, Ramirez sits down at his keyboards and begins to play a Bach sonata. He looks so content that David can hardly believe it's the same person who only moments ago was a madman violently attacking him, and intent on destroying the world just to prove a point.

Maybe he'll stop, David hopes, *at least for the Millennium celebration. But in case he doesn't, I'd better be prepared to stop him myself, using the tools that Rami gave me. And God, I hope I do it right. Or I might be the one to blow up Port Avalon.*

Twenty-eight

As David plays them on his computer keyboard and watches the colorful patterns dance across the monitor, every musical scale resonates deep inside him. Rami's words resound clearly in his head: *"Music... is a symbol of what you, yourself, are made of, what you are capable of. Once you tap into the Triune Power... you will touch the face of God... and put an end to Ramirez's unholy scheme."*

David then moves from one instrument to another. He sits pensively at the precious old grand piano in the Nickerson family parlor. One of the oldest polyphonic instruments created, with an unprecedented capacity to transform the ten fingers of a pianist into a creator of multiple melodies and rhythms at once, the piano is superior in David's mind to the dazzling complexities of today's electronic keyboards. Each tone is pure and one of a kind, its beauty and power reliant on the craftsmanship of the piano maker and string tuner.

David runs his hands along each of the 88 keys. Oh, if he could only hear the sound of each one resonate in the air, filling the room with a poignant ambience. This is a memory he carries within him, from the years before he lost his hearing, of his mother seated at this very same piano playing Brahms, Chopin and Strauss in a passionate interpretation of her own.

So, this is where my love of music began, and why I continue to pursue it to this day. Is this how Beethoven felt after his hearing went? How impertinent I am, David thinks, *to ever equate himself in any way with*

Beethoven. Then he remembers something Dr. Ramirez told him: "You hear *inner* music, David. Not everyone does." Perhaps - no, no perhaps about it. This is definitely what Beethoven heard: inner music when the outer music disappeared into a tunnel of deafness.

Taking in the expanse of the piano's width, some pertinent descriptions from David's music theory books loom large:

The piano has 88 keys: 7 black keys and 5 white keys, which make an octave, an interval of 8 tones. From the left to the right of the keyboard are 16 of these octaves, which reduce numerically to 7. The 12 black and white keys comprise the 12 semi-tones of the chromatic scale.

Most people are familiar with the diatonic major scales heard in today's music - *do, re, mi, fa, so, la, ti, do* - the first 7 notes that span a full octave with 5 full tones and 2 half tones, ending on the final *do* (8th note), which is a repeat of the first *do*, only an octave higher tonally. For example, a basic octave scale of notes on the piano would be written on a music score as: *c, d, e, f, g, a, b, c*).

Somewhere in these keys, these octaves, these tones, is the key to the puzzle of those cryptic messages that pop up on David's computer screen. Music, he has learned, is more than just notes and scales; these notes and scales mean something mysterious as well as mathematical.

"Mathematical! Yes!" The light goes on in his memory again. "Now where are my books on Pythagoras?" - the master Greek mathematician (550 B.C.) who gave a scientific basis to the diatonic music scale upon which most of Western music is based.

But more than just a master at the science of numbers and mathematics, Pythagoras believed that the 7 music tones of the diatonic scale correlated to the Divine Music of the Spheres (the 7 planets of the solar system), and to the 7 Spirits before the Throne of God. Many people have believed for centuries that, in using the Pythagorean principles in their music, master composers such as Mozart and Beethoven were creating music channeled from a divine source and not just from their own brain.

But there are 12 tones, David calculates, *in each of the 16 octaves on the piano, which reduce to 7...*

"That's it!" David yells. "12 is 7 is... but where is the 5 and the 3? 12 is 7 is 5 is 3... where are the other numbers? And what do they mean anyway! Rats! Think!"

No, don't overthink. Remember what Dorinda told me when I was held hostage in the Prism Palace by the evil High Priestess Jaycina: *"Listen... listen to its song... listen to what it's trying to tell you..."*

"But," David recalls now, "that was when I had the Singer. She wanted me to hold it in my hand and listen to what it was telling me. Of course. How dumb I am!"

He rushes to his room and retrieves the precious Singer crystal from its pouch, the Singer that Rami had saved and protected until he could return it to David, its rightful owner. He carries it downstairs and sits at the piano. Holding the crystal with one hand and placing his other gently over a span of white and black keys, he listens, and hears...

Black symbolizes spiritual power in latency; White symbolizes spiritual power in manifestation. Music being the first of the arts, shall also be the last - the alpha and the omega, the highest and most important of them all.

Twenty-nine

David now has the Singer crystal, and understands its purpose in his current mission. But what is he to do about the Rose Crystal? He wants to put it around Sally's neck to see if it will heal her. But Rami insisted that David has something to do before he can. *But what is it? And when will I know?*

Upstairs, David passes by his Aunt Dorothy's room. He so wants to talk with her, but she tires so easily that he resists the temptation to use her as a sounding board. Instead, he walks to his sister's room and goes in, wanting to get one of her stuffed animals to bring to her in the hospital. He sees her diary on the desk and certainly doesn't want to read it, but it is open to a page that bears David's name...

"Oh, how I wish David would have an operation so that he could hear again. Then maybe he would stay with us and not need to go on his adventures on the Moon Singer. Wherever it is that he goes, he can hear other people, and beautiful music, and I know he wants to stay there.

"He thinks he can make me walk again normally, and he says he sees and talks to Mom when he's away. How can we compete with those miracles? So I won't help him with Dad. I won't ever tell Dad that I believe David can do all those things. I know they fight and it's so hard, but maybe I can make David see that this is where he belongs. If only he would have that surgery..."

David is shocked to think that he has been so selfish, even though he thought he was being helpful to his sister, hoping that by using his crystals he could help her to wake up from her coma and walk again. He has no choice now.

* * *

Isaac is surprised that David has finally agreed to have the cochlear implant. He had been so adamant, so dead set against it.

"I'm really happy that you've decided on the surgery, David. But what made you change your mind?"

"I think it's what Sally wants. Maybe it will help her wake up if I can talk to her, and hear her, normally."

"If so, it will be the best Christmas present she could ever have, the best present for all of us."

* * *

David has been here before, at Dr. Jabbour's office for treatment decisions, supplements, new hearing aids, and discussions of surgical options.

"I didn't think I'd see you here again, David," the doctor says. "You've been disappointed with everything we've done so far."

"Yes, I have," David concurs, "but I thought maybe I was being selfish. It's hard for my family to deal with all of this."

"Just to be clear, David, you have to do this for yourself. There are no guarantees with a cochlear implant. You have to want to hear normally, and to be willing to take the risk of surgery. But you couldn't be a better candidate. So, I have high hopes for you."

"My dad feels guilty. He said I could be deaf because of him, because it runs in his family and even though the deafness skipped him, I inherited his genes."

"Well, that's a very small part of the equation, David," Dr. Jabbour reassures his patient. "You were fortunate not to have been born deaf and to have had several years of normal hearing, which is why you speak so well. But you also had a couple of double whammies here. Not just the gene pool, but you did have a terrible bout of meningitis, and otosclerosis caused profound sensorineural hearing loss in both ears. But you have had some success with the new high tech hearing aids. And I must say, I'm proud of the way you learned to read lips and sign."

"Thanks, Doc. Thanks to my mom, and my sister, who spent weeks and months learning to sign with me. So, I did have lots of family support."

"Well, you're going to need all the support you can get after the surgery, too. Okay, David. I've got you all scheduled for Monday. So rest up this weekend and let's get you hearing for Christmas."

Thirty

David will sleep peacefully for several hours under a general anesthetic while Dr. Jabbour surgically implants a device that everyone hopes will give him normal hearing once again.

First, a small area of David's scalp directly behind his ear is shaved and cleaned. An incision is made in the skin and Dr. Jabbour then drills into his mastoid bone, creating a pocket for the receiver/stimulator, and then another incision into David's inner ear where the electrode array is inserted into the cochlea.

The receiver/stimulator, once secured into bone beneath the skin, will convert the signals into electric impulses and send them through an internal cable to electrodes that are wound through the cochlea. This allows impulses to be sent directly to the brain through the auditory nerve system.

Externally, the implanted device consists of a microphone which picks up sounds from the environment, and a speech processor which selectively filters sounds, splits them into channels and sends the signals through a thin cable to a transmitter. The transmitter itself is a coil held in position by a magnet placed behind David's ear.

As with every medical procedure, this surgery involves a certain amount of risk including possible skin infections, the onset of tinnitus - ringing in the ear - damage to the vestibular system which affects movement and balance, and damage to facial nerves that can cause muscle weakness, impaired facial sensation, and worst of all, facial paralysis. Complete device failure is also a possibility in rare instances. These potential risks, and the destruction of some residual hearing that David might have, is why Dr. Jabbour advised only single-ear implantation, thereby saving his other ear in case a biological treatment becomes available in the future.

Being a strong and healthy young man, David comes through the surgery itself quite well and is able to go home the same day. With each passing day, David's hearing improves and he shows no signs of complications resulting from the surgery. But as his hearing gets progressively better, what he hears is painful and annoying.

The chattering sound of voices interrupt his contemplation and concentration. A door slamming, a window shutter banging in the winter wind, motorcycles, trucks, all the clatter disturb his inner silence and he wishes he could shut it off, preferring the silence to the din of everyday life.

"*How do people stand it day in and day out, hour after hour?*" he wonders.

The worst disappointment of all is hearing the raucous music playing on the radio, the discord and confusion of sounds being labeled "music" is not what he wants to hear. He begins to understand why Dr. Ramirez is so disenchanted and has such disdain for music's evolution - or is it *regression?* - that he would fall prey to its destructive potential. Saliana's music is what David wants to hear. That sweet, angelic, celestial sound. But will he ever hear it again now that he has had the surgery?

Will the Moon Singer ever call to him again? Will he ever again sail on the silent rivers of moonbeams and stars, as Captain at the helm of the exquisite clipper ship? Sailing her has tranquility about it, Saliana had told him: "*You could never hear what you need to hear if jet engines were roaring all around you.*"

But jet engines are all around him now, and fog horns and car horns, trash trucks and the aggravating beep of car alarms late at night. Yet, he will withstand all the agony if it helps Sally get well.

* * *

David brings the Rose Crystal pendant with him to Sally in the hospital, hoping that the moment will arise when he can place it around her neck. He sits by her side, and talks to her quietly and sincerely.

"Hi, Sal. Well, I did it. I had the operation like you wanted and I can hear. I can hear everything. And I want to hear your voice, too. If you will just wake up we can finally talk to each other, like we did when we were little kids - with no sign language or reading lips. Come on, Sal. I know you can hear me. Somewhere deep inside you, you know I'm here."

David takes the Rose Crystal Pendant from his pocket ready to place it around her neck, when he hesitates, realizing that he can't do it just yet. There is some mission he must complete, at Rami's urging, before he can use the pendant to help his sister. *Was it to have the surgery? Was that the important thing I had to do first?*

Instinctively, he knows it is not; he knows that whatever major assignment Rami entrusted him to complete was not something that would benefit himself. If only Rami hadn't been so vague, so reticent to tell David exactly in plain words what the heck it was!

Reluctantly, David puts the necklace back in his pocket. Surprisingly, Sally stirs. He talks to her some more.

"Sal! That's it. Are you waking up? You know you can. Just try. Try really hard. I'm here for you..."

With an indistinguishable murmur on her lips, Sally moves her head slightly, takes a small breath, and flutters her eyes a bit.

"Come on, Sal. A little more. Please don't go back to sleep!" David coaxes her.

"Da - vid?" Her voice is ever so weak, but audible.

"Yes, Sal. It's me. David. And I can hear you just like you heard me."

Sally opens her eyes to see David sitting by her bedside, with tears streaming down his face. "Don't cry, David. Don't...It's not your fault..."

Sally's nurse comes rushing in and checks her vital signs, then rings for the Charge Nurse to call her doctor.

Sally's eyes close again, but she is stirring, and lifting her hand toward her brother. David takes her hand in his and holds it tightly.

"She's coming back, isn't she,"David implores the nurse.

"Yes, just a little. But it's a good sign. The doctor will give her a thorough exam when he gets here."

"I'll call my dad and let him know."

* * *

It's not all that Isaac had hoped for. Sally didn't fully wake for several days and she is still too week to leave the hospital. But he couldn't have asked for a better Christmas present than to have his daughter back and his son hearing normally.

"I have a gift for you, Son." Isaac hands David a small box wrapped with only a red ribbon. David opens it and is stunned at what is inside.

"But, Dad, you can't give me grandfather's watch fob. It's your most precious possession."

"You and Sally are my most precious possessions. I thought it was about time that I passed this heirloom on to you. You've been through so much and I haven't always been there for you. But I am now, and always will be."

David and Isaac hug tightly, intensely, both teary-eyed with emotion. But before things become too sentimental, the doorbell rings. It is David who hears it and proceeds to open the door.

"Hello, David," Janice greets him. "Merry Christmas. May I come in?"

"Of course you can. You're always welcome here, isn't she Dad?"

Isaac stares at the woman he loves standing in the foyer, but hesitates to greet her too warmly, still stinging from the rebuke she gave him at that disastrous dinner they shared with Bianca Creighton

"I wanted to apologize to you for the way I acted. I don't really know what came over me and I don't expect you to fully understand just yet. I don't think I do, frankly. But I couldn't let this Christmas go by without being here, and sharing your happiness about Sally and David."

Isaac takes Janice's hand and escorts her into the living room. "I'm glad you're here, Jan. I don't think I could get through all of this without you by my side."

Thirty-one

The Millennium celebration is at a feverish pitch. Some of the more optimistic people are dancing, singing, and drinking in the town square, ready to ring in the most momentous New Year of their lifetime, the dawn of not just another century but of another thousand years.

The fear mongers are out proselytizing, still trying to cash in during the last few hours of December, selling Millennium Survival Kits or soliciting donations to a particular religious movement that promises a rapturous eternity when the world ends!

The fearful are praying or staying home, bracing for the worst.

In his room, David works on his computer entering the codes that Rami gave him to infiltrate Dr. Ramirez's music programs. In no time at all, David is into the professor's system. Knowing exactly what to look for he scans the files and comes up with two critical documents. One file contains the devastating musical configurations Ramirez created that can trigger any type of climatic disaster of his choosing. The other file describes the weather satellites that Ramirez can hack into to wreak havoc on the world. If a terrorist were to discover these codes, the entire world could be held hostage indefinitely.

David's own instinct is to delete the files, erase them completely from Ramirez's computer. But he is certain that Ramirez copied the files to another computer or to a disk, and hid them somewhere for safe keeping. David also knows that Rami is right: the formulas themselves must be neutralized entirely, so that they could never be used by Ramirez nor ever discovered by anyone else even more wicked.

* * *

Twenty-four hours a day, the news is overwhelming with reports of major storms around the world: a blizzard in the Midwestern United States, a whiteout in Canada; vicious floods in Asia and Europe; winds measured at more than 200 mph blowing small towns apart and killing hundreds; Tsunamis washing away vulnerable, primitive villages.

David knows that a calamity in Port Avalon is imminent, and he must act decisively before it occurs. To complicate matters, Dr. Ramirez has been consigned by the Town Council to create a special musical interlude for the clock tower chimes to play in celebration of the Millennium. Knowing Ramirez and his shrewd mind, David intuits just when that might be. What better time for inflicting a monumental disaster than when everyone is gathered in the town square watching the countdown of the Millennium clock?

It is there that David must perform a Herculean feat, one similar to his destruction of the Glass Snake on the Island of Darkness, using the Singer as a conduit...

He had been successful in rescuing Saliana from the Tower of the Prism Palace, and outwitting the High Priestess Jaycina to the point that he and Saliana could escape her clutches and her wrath. They were able to find the secret door leading out of the Palace and ran for their lives to freedom.

But the Glass Snake was in hot pursuit, thundering across the Palace grounds toward them. He moved quickly on massive clawed feet, despite the stubby thickness of his legs. His powerful gait shook the ground, nearly knocking David and Saliana off their balance. They scrambled to the pedestal at the mouth of the Volcano that swallowed men up whole at Jaycina's command, and climbed up on it. The Snake was mere yards away, his wild eyes two red mirrors of doom. Saliana shrieked hysterically.

David was unexpectedly struck with a sharp, searing pain in his ear and he flattened his hands over his ears to subdue it. But, the pain then turned into an unbearable ringing and David abruptly pulled his hearing aid out, cutting off all the sounds of panic that surrounded him. As he did so, the din became a hum, then a soothing hush, like the tranquil ebb and flow of the ocean tides he loved so much. Immersed in this secure cocoon, David realized instinctively what he must do and reached into his tunic for the Singer crystal. He held it high, like a cross of "good" opposing the forces of evil.

Instantly, the Singer was ignited with the crackling energy emanating from the Glass Volcano and emitted a dazzling, prismatic spray of multi-colored light, which then emblazoned the Star of David that Ishtar has sewn onto David's tunic with powerful crystal beads.

"His tail, David. Cut off his tail and he will die!" David remembers the command of the doomed Judiah, the traitor who was seconds away from death in the abyss of the hungry Volcano.

David pointed the Singer toward the Snake's tail and the little crystal clipper spewed out a hail of incendiary sparks. The reptile's scaly tail exploded into a million pieces, sending fragments of shattering multi-colored glass into the sky like a Fourth of July fireworks display. The Snake roared violently, one final gasp for life before the instant of death, then collapsed in a thunderous heap.

In the explosion, a glorious burst of light hurtled through the sky like a meteor toward the Moon Singer. The energy hit the gallant clipper ship's railing, slithered along the conduit Ishtar had fashioned from the gold rings that encircled the great ship's masts, and connected to the clipper's mizzenmast full force. Her sails burst open and, regaining full power, the Moon Singer began to glide magically on the water.

Ishtar had run up and down the main deck, whooping victoriously, as a misty spray of water washed away his grateful tears. "You did it, David! You did it. You remembered, my boy. You remembered..."

And now, on this fateful last day of the century, to defeat the evil that is Dr. Ramirez and to save the lives of everyone he loves, David must *remember* what his mission is, how he is to complete it, and use the knowledge he has been given by divine forces.

* * *

The moment is only a few hours away.

But before he can hone the enormous task clearly in his mind, he must pay a New Year's Eve visit to Sally and see if she still feels as she did when she wrote those painful words in her diary, wishing David could hear so that he would never leave home again.

When David arrives, she is sitting up in a chair, which is a promising and a pleasant sight. They greet each other warmly, and for a few moments she is the Sally he remembers from a few months ago.

Sally touches his ear and examines the cochlear implant receiver that now allows her brother to talk to her without sign language and to hear perfectly without having to read her lips. She is amazed and yet puzzled.

"I did it for you, Sal," David tells her. "For us. I felt so alone without you while you were in your coma. And so guilty, too."

"Why should you feel guilty? It's not your fault you can't hear - or couldn't, that is."

"Are you sure you don't think it was my fault? I - I read your diary," he confesses, and adds quickly, "I didn't mean to. I went into your room to get Peter Rabbit for you," he says referring to the stuffed animal she holds to comfort herself, a ritual she has performed since childhood. "The diary was just open to a page where you wrote how angry you were with me for going on my Moon Singer adventures. To places where I could hear."

"Yes, I was angry. Oh, I know I loved hearing about it all when it was our little secret."

"So what changed, Sal?"

"When you came back that second time and kept talking about how you saw Mom, and I just was so mad. I didn't want it to be true, that you could see her and I couldn't. So I told myself that none of what you had done was true. That you made it all up."

"But, Sal, you know how my crystals and my adventures helped you. When I came back from the Island the first time, you could walk."

"Yes, and I was so happy. But it didn't last long. You could hear, too, but that didn't last long either."

David nods his head in understanding. "No it didn't."

"But I didn't mind that I couldn't walk without crutches or braces," Sally says, emotion building up in her voice. "Until you decided you had to go back. You left us again to be with other people. People you said you loved! Not us! I missed you so..."

She starts to sob and David holds her hand tightly, and wipes her tears away with a tissue.

"I know, I know. I missed you, too. But when I came back I found the Rose Crystal again and it worked some magic again, didn't it? Remember how you and I danced together at my birthday party?"

"That was just a dream, David. Just a dream. Something we only wanted to happen. Just like saying you saw Mom!"

"But I did, Sally, I promise you I did!"

"Mom's dead, David. She's never coming back no matter how many crazy experiments you do with your crystals!"

...and the fairy tale daydreams have served their purpose. His mother's heart is now wide open to embrace and guide his path to discovery...dig more deeply, David...

He holds his weeping sister in his arms and makes a promise he vows to keep. "If it's in my power, Sal, I'll make sure you and Mom see each other again, so you can have a chance to say goodbye one last time."

Thirty-two

With the Singer crystal, the Rose Crystal and the Wind Rose Compass close at hand, David prepares to position himself in the town square's clock tower. At last David knows what that mysterious numeric notation displayed on his computer monitor time after time signifies: 12 is 7 is 5 is 3, is a sacred cryptogram that, when arranged in the correct numerological sequence, will give David the exact time when he should engage the three sacred artifacts in his possession. At that precise moment, they will defuse Ramirez's destructive musical composition forever.

David reviews in his mind what each artifact symbolizes:

THE SINGER: The little Singer Crystal, the one sculpted into a miniature replica of the Moon Singer, was long ago programmed by very wise men with all the knowledge of the universe, with the answers to all the mysteries contemplated by humankind. Used as the apex in a crystal grid, it acts as a conduit to ignite the power of all the other crystals in the pattern.

When David first experimented with the Star of David grid pattern on the Port Avalon beach that summer afternoon, little did he know then that each point of the six-pointed Star had its own unique role to play in the life of the seeker: Mercy, Power, Justice, Love, Truth, Wisdom. These last three comprise the Trinity Symbol, a small perfect triangle engraved by Ishtar on the primary facet of the Singer, serving as a doorway into its powerful wisdom. The Trinity symbol cannot be easily seen by just anyone. One must hold the crystal up to a bright light while closely examining all of its facets. Bianca knew that someday, when he was ready, David would discover this symbol himself. And now, because of his persistent pursuit of knowledge, he has.

THE ROSE CRYSTAL: The beautiful Rose Crystal is imbued with Saliana's healing song, music so perfect it has the power of physical healing and spiritual immortality. No wonder the monstrous Glass Snake coveted this treasure. Its gifts would heal its evil heart and give it everlasting life. But in truth it was the High Priestess Jaycina who coveted the gem for herself, while perpetrating the hoax of the Glass Snake to provoke fear and intimidation into the hearts and minds of the inhabitants of the Island of Darkness. In saving Saliana, David saved the Rose Crystal pendant from Jaycina's malevolent clutches and brought a miracle home to his sister. And now that Saliana has programmed it with David's soul code, it will play a monumental role in healing Sally completely, and saving Port Avalon and the world from utter destruction.

THE WIND ROSE: Though to some the Wind Rose is merely an ancient compass, its 32 points resemble a beautiful flower. Its North point was originally represented by a *fleur-de-lis* for the veteran mariner, but for the soul traveler, the *fleur-de-lis* was replaced by a cross, meant to point the way to Paradise. For David, "paradise" is exemplified as service to others. And it is through his possession of the Wind Rose that he has been able to come to this realization, a recognition of purpose that it takes some people years - lifetimes - to experience.

Yet the sacred compass is unique in that its power is a double-edged sword: in knowing hands it is capable of immense destruction, as happened in Coronadus when Bianca used the Wind Rose to destroy her beloved city to save the children from the greed and hostilities that threatened their future; and in trusted hands, the Wind Rose breathes life into dormant spiritual longings just as, when in David's hands, it stirred the wind to life again in Coronadus after a long siege of stillness and stagnation and allowed him to awaken the Moon Singer and to sail her home again.

THE MOON SINGER: The magnificent clipper ship Moon Singer is the manifestation of all that the three sacred artifacts promise. In her giant masts made of crystal is the source of all the knowledge found in the Singer, for it was from a piece of the mizzenmast the Singer was sculpted. Encased in the gold rings encircling the three masts is the same Trinity symbol that was carved onto the Singer's facet, thereby rendering them one and the same.

The Moon Singer was conjured up by David who heard Saliana's celestial song. The ship transported him to other times and places, where the past, present and future were one. She tested him and protected him from harm. And when his mission was accomplished, she brought him safely home.

And yet, the Moon Singer has a mission of her own, one so profound that her presence will be felt all around the world in just moments from now.

* * *

Because of his ownership of the three powerful artifacts, and because of the rapidity of his spiritual evolution, David is entrusted with another mission, one so enormously critical to everyone he loves, to his home town, and to the world itself, that he cannot falter or fail. If he succeeds everyone will benefit, and the Moon Singer will reappear. Will he be compelled to board the magnificent sailing ship one more time, see her sails billow out in a breathtaking expanse of silky white clouds? Or will this be the last time David's sees her? Will anyone else see her majestic presence? Or will he still be the only one?

If he fails...

But he dare not even think of failure or its consequences.

Knowing the precise time that the professor will set off a chain of cataclysmic events, David is to arrange the three sacred pieces in a triangular formation. At the fateful moment, when the big clock's minute hand moves to the 59th minute of the 11th hour, and the second hand ticks the 59th second of the final minute of the century, the sound will resonate through each point of the triangle. The combined musical vibrations of the Singer, the Rose Crystal, and the Wind Rose compass will cause the earth and the universe to stand still. The Power of Three will become One, and what will be heard is the divine Cosmic Chord, the chord that sounded in the heavens the day that the world was created.

There will be no destruction that day. Every disaster will be thwarted, every attempt by Dr. Ramirez to enact his revenge on a perceived enemy will not come to fruition. The Moon Singer will appear, her glorious visage will light up the sky and mark the dawn of a new age.

As long as David remembers what he is to do and why he is to do it.

Thirty-three

It is 11:30pm. He has less than 30 minutes to accomplish his task. As briskly as he can, David climbs the stairs - all 20 floors - of the clock tower. Of course, the elevator would be easier and quicker, but he prefers no one see him. Without authorization, no one is permitted to access the top of the tower. People rarely take the stairs and he was counting on that tonight.

But he didn't count on one person in particular.

Moving stealthily in the shadows behind him, Dr. Ramirez climbs the hundreds of steps. Obviously not as young or agile as David, he is a few minutes and a few flights behind. It is pure coincidence that Ramirez and David are ascending the clock tower at the same time. The professor has malevolent motives for being there; he can't imagine why his protégé would be there at the same time.

Nonetheless, Ramirez is cautious and quite curious to see what David is up to. Perhaps, Ramirez thinks, David is just a typical college kid, acting on a dare from his peers to get some video of the Millennium Ball from above as it drops. Whatever the reason, David's presence will interfere with Ramirez's plan.

Finally, David reaches the top floor. He stops to catch his breath. Ramirez is just behind him, and comes through the access door to confront a startled David.

"What are you doing here, Doc?"

"I might ask you the same thing, David. I have permission to be here, to be sure my music chip will play on time when the ball drops. No one else has been authorized to be up here with me. So you'd better go before someone catches you."

With time running out, David has no choice but to tell the truth. It's too late to mince words and use psychology on a man who is truly demented and hell bent on carrying out a horrendous act of terrorism.

"I'm sorry Professor. I can't leave you here alone. I know what you've been doing and I'm here to stop you from doing any further harm."

"Really, David. I don't know what you're talking about. What kind of nonsense is in your head?"

"It's not nonsense. I know all about your music codes and the havoc you've been wreaking around the world. I won't let you destroy Port Avalon, too."

"You foolish boy! You know nothing about the world, and even less about the work I've been doing! It's too late for you to stop me now. You're neither strong enough nor clever enough." Ramirez checks his watch to see that he has only moments to execute his final plan.

"I don't want to hurt you, David, but if you won't leave willingly I'll have to make you leave." He grabs David by the arm and tries to force him out the door so he can lock him out. But David pulls free and starts to overpower his mentor. Ramirez in turn pushes David as hard as he can, knocking his head against the wall. Stunned, David slumps down to the floor, blood trickling down his head from the blow.

Ramirez threatens that he has created a new music sequence that is even more deadly than the one that David stole from his computer.

Struggling to his feet, David warns him he will not get a chance to use it.

Ramirez reveals a remote device that will go off at 11:59:59pm, just one minute from now. His finger moves onto the button. One quick push and it's all over.

"No! Don't!" David yells. He swipes at Ramirez to grab the device. The professor loses his balance trying to hold on to the palm size detonator, but he loses his grip and the detonator drops swiftly over the side and down toward the ground. Frantically grabbing at it, Ramirez falls head first over the railing.

David tries desperately to grab onto his mentor hoping to save him from the fall as well as from himself. He grabs at the professor's jacket. Holding on for dear life, David feels himself teetering over the edge. His right hand strains to maintain its grip on the smooth leather sleeve, while his left hand frantically grabs onto the rail trying to pull him back to safety.

There is nothing he can do.

David stands helplessly with the torn jacket in his hand as the screaming Ramirez drops 20 floors, his arms and legs flailing in terror, his screams unheard in the hubbub of New Year's Eve on Main Street in Port Avalon.

Thirty-four

At precisely 11:59:59 pm in Port Avalon, darkness comes at the same time to all nations and all time zones. The sun has retired itself, the moon has curtained its light demurely with slow-moving clouds, and the stars have dimmed behind an ethereal haze.

To most, this change in the environment merely denotes the transition from day to night. And they eagerly anticipate the hour of midnight when they will join together around the world to celebrate a new era for mankind. They do not consciously note that all corners of the globe are experiencing the same phenomenon, the obliteration of time zones. They are all too caught up in their own local revelry to see that time has stood still at 11:59:59 pm.

David has climbed to the top of the clock tower, with the three sacred pieces in hand. He has placed them in a triangular formation with the Singer at the Apex. His heart beats wildly with trepidation. He must do something that is purely intuitive. In a split second, he must remember exactly what he did to destroy the Glass Snake, escape the evils of the High Priestess Jaycina, save Saliana's life and in turn save his sister Sally from a cruel limbo.

Just as he experienced on that fateful last day on the Island of Darkness, David is unexpectedly struck with a sharp, searing pain in his ear. The pain becomes an unbearable ringing and David reaches up instinctively. But on this night there is no hearing aid to pull out that will silence all the sounds of impending climatic destruction that hovers over Port Avalon. On this night there is only the instrument that allows him to hear in his "real" world of family and everyday responsibilities. There is only the cochlear implant that separates him from this world and the "other" world where he can hear without a hearing aid or any other device; where he can experience a blissful serenity, and the past, present and future as one; where there is no judgment or criticism, but there is exhilaration in the revelation as to who he is and what he was meant to become.

And so, in that last second before the almost unbelievable changes to occur, David moves the three artifacts into their synergistic position, and in doing so the implant's receiver is disabled. The din of celebration becomes a hum, then a soothing hush, like the tranquil ebb and flow of the ocean tides he loves so much. Just as on that auspicious day on the Port Avalon beach, where he aligned his crystals in the Star of David Grid with the Singer at the apex, and Saliana's song beckoned him to a world unknown, what he hears now will change his life forever.

Immersed in this secure and familiar cocoon, it is not someone else's music that he hears, not Saliana's or Beethoven's or any of the great masters of divine music. What David hears is his soul code, the music that pulses in his brain, in his DNA, in his heart. And all becomes clear: the voices he hears and the messages they impart, are those of his own inner intuitions and yearnings.

"I can't think of any words to describe this moment."

Other: There are no words needed.

"Just the music of his soul. He hears it calling and it resonates out to those he loves."

Other: He is so close, so close to knowing, to understanding.

"All he needs to do is let it play out."

Other: And recognize it as his own.

Thirty-five

One second later, when the Big Ball denoting the New Year descends, it is not the customary New Year's Ball constructed of a mere 100 incandescent light bulbs, iron, and wood. In its new incarnation it glows with 1000 multicolored LED lights and an outer surface consisting of triangle-shaped crystal panels.

Simultaneously, the three mysterious images that people have been seeing for months in the far corners of the earth transform into enormous rings, towering masts, and a titanic hull. They move toward each other gracefully, then blend into one distinct image to become the Moon Singer.

"And how shall I come to earth this time - in what form and in which incarnation..."

She arrives in a river of diamonds and Pearls, a winged spirit of angelic vision, a magnificent light, the light of the eternal soul, almost too bright for human eyes. *The face of God?* David wonders. *Is that what this beautiful ship really is?*

Then the Voice comes from everywhere and nowhere:

"You have brought yourself to the brink, with unprecedented innovation, creativity, vision and skill, but you also have broken every universal law of cause and effect, without regard to the consequences. Over and over again you have chosen war over peace, violence over compassion, and greed over benevolence. And you suffer because you have not learned.

God did not cause your misfortune, but neither could God stop it, for in having free will the choices that are good for one will hurt another. You've lost your sense of mystery and wonder. To find it again, you must go back to the Source. Each of you must discover the secret of life for yourself. Get it? Your mistakes will repeat over and over again until you Get it!"

"Get it!" Isaac repeats. "That's what Bianca Creighton said."

"As long as there are people, there will be conflict," the Voice continues, as if from loud speakers mounted on every corner of the earth and the heavens, *"but if everyone with a peaceful heart lifted up a lantern of love at the same time, evil would be forever dimmed, and infinite good would shine brighter than human eyes could bear on this earth. This is why the Light is shown only to those who reach the portals of Heaven itself."*

Isaac turns to someone in the crowd. A familiar energy attracts him to a woman with her back turned. She senses his approach and turns to face him.

"Dr. Creighton?" Isaac addresses her.

Bianca removes her head scarf and her golden blonde hair tumbles about her shoulders, wisping sensuously in the cool breeze. In unison, David and Isaac gasp as they each see someone they never expected to see again on this earth.

"Mom?" David whispers, thunderstruck.

"Billie?" Isaac calls her.

"I am all of them. I am all of you," she pronounces gently. "I've come to ease your heart and to say goodbye. Quickly now, there isn't much time!"

Thirty-six

"But where are we going?" David asks, as Bianca hustles him and his father along through the crowd.

"I don't understand. I thought you were back in the Kingdom with Ishtar and Saliana."

"I came back with you, to be sure you got home okay and that all went as planned."

David thinks a second then is offended. "Wait. You mean you came back to – to spy on me?"

"Good heavens, David. No. I didn't come back to spy on you or make sure you performed your task well. I knew you would."

"Then, why? I'm really puzzled as to why you are letting Dad see you!"

"He sees me, but he doesn't really. I know it's complicated but he'll be with us, experiencing everything you and I do, and then forget pretty much what he saw. He'll think it's all a dream."

"You can do that?"

"No. He'll do it for himself. Now get a move on so we can see Sally. We have but a few moments before I must return home."

"Home. You mean the Kingdom. Is - is everything okay? I didn't screw things up again, did I?"

"No, dear boy. All is well in the Kingdom of Light because you have made everything right in Port Avalon. Now we must make everything right with Sally."

* * *

She is sitting up in bed when they arrive at the hospital, but is in a drowsy twilight sleep. Bianca's breath catches when she sees her sweet daughter, Sally. For this moment, she is now Billie Nickerson, Sally and David's mother, and Isaac's departed wife. She takes Sally's hand in hers and the girl's eyes open.

It takes a few seconds for the vision before her to resonate in Sally's brain. Then the full realization hits her. Standing before her is her beloved mother, the mother she lost in a horrible accident not so long ago. But how? How can this be?

"You can't be here...this is a dream. I'm not really seeing you, am I – Mom?"

"Yes, dearest. You are seeing me. You and David and your father."

"But I thought only David could see you. David," she beseeches her brother, "are we all off on one of your Moon Singer fantasies? Please don't do this to me. It's too cruel."

Sally begins to cry and Billie embraces her, holding her fast and rocking her back and forth. "There, now. Don't cry. It's not a fantasy, Sally. It's me. It's Mom. I've come back one more time to help you understand what happened to me, and to ease any painful thoughts you have, any guilt you carry. Only then can all of you say goodbye and truly move on with your lives."

"No, Mom, no! Please don't come back just to leave us again! Please." Sally is sobbing now.

Billie smoothes her daughter's hair back tenderly, and wipes the tears from her cheeks. "It will all be all right, Sweetest. Trust me."

Billie then turns to Isaac and holds him near. Hesitantly at first, Isaac returns the embrace. Then, feeling her familiar warmth, he holds her passionately. After a lingering moment, Billie steps back and looks deep into his eyes, those sympathetic brown eyes that now concern her.

"My dear husband, love of my life. It pains me so to know that you, more than anyone, carry such a deep burden of guilt in your heart.

It was not your fault that foggy night that changed all of our lives instantly. It was just what it was, an accident. It had nothing to do with your rushing to get your designs in on deadline. It was fate that it was just my time."

"Your time!" Isaac's voice cracks with anguish. "What about Sally? Was it her time to be crippled forever?"

"I know you can't understand this now, but I think David and Sally will. Her injuries served a higher good, for both of them. But it will all be over soon. Sally will walk again, if David has anything to do with it."

Billie turns to her son. "David, my precious, gifted, extraordinary boy. Life holds so much promise for you and for everyone you love, if you continue to fulfill your mission. I know it is a lot to ask of someone so young, and you were thrown into it unwittingly. But now you have conscious awareness of who you are and what you are meant to do."

"Everyone keeps saying that," David replies, partly confused and angry, partly acquiescent. "I guess I don't have much choice but to go along."

She holds David's hand and take's Isaac's in the other, and tells David to take Sally's hand, so they form a complete circle.

"My dear, precious family. I have missed you so much. I will always miss you. But it is time to say a final farewell. Know that I will always be with you, as you are with me."

Billie's image, encircled by Bianca's glowing aura, disappears into the ethers, and with her any memory Isaac and Sally might have of this moment.

David will never forget.

Thirty-seven

The New Millennium

Not everyone who experienced the Vision accepted it as a good omen. They went back to their normal way of living, being cynical and superstitious of everything and everyone. They thought it was some kind of trick, a New Year's Eve hallucination created by some tech savvy jokesters, mainly because there was no video or photo that captured even one frame of the image.

Others became more tolerant and loving, believing they had seen a vision from "on high," something angelic. Still others refused to acknowledge there was any vision at all.

"Don't be silly," they scoffed. "Angels can't morph into objects or people, if angels even exist at all." To them, it was nothing more than the normal descent of the illuminated ball, marking the end of one year and the start of another.

At the stroke of Midnight marking the New Millennium, none of the terrible things people feared would happen, happened. No computers crashed, no violence occurred, no disasters manifested. Worldwide, people came together in unity and love, tolerance, and an unbridled celebration of life. Any tragedies that occurred did so before that 12th stroke of the clock, and would be remembered as history, remnants of a previous year, a bygone century.

As usual, the TV news media focused on the sensational and the absurd. Over and over again, they replayed an ironic video showing a man falling from the clock tower terrace and landing on an expansive canvas awning that broke his fall. With each bounce Ramirez took on the taut cloth, a silly sound effect would accent the rhythm.

"Amazingly," newscasters reported satirically, "the man only suffered abrasions and a broken clavicle, but otherwise will recover fully. At least, physically.

"When asked how he came to fall," the story went, "he said he was waiting to take pictures of the ball drop at the stroke of midnight, when a UFO in the shape of a clipper ship appeared in the sky, startled him, and his camera fell out of his hands. He tried to reach for it and, that was that. It was a miracle that he fell onto the awning of the Town Square restaurant. His camera was not so lucky; a passerby found it smashed to bits after a delivery truck ran over it."

Or what they thought was a camera.

"Needless to say," the news stated, "the man, identified as Professor Ramirez of Port Avalon City College, is being held over for psychiatric observation."

* * *

At home in her room, Dorothy Nickerson had watched the festivities of the Millennium celebration on television. As the shimmering miracle of the Moon Singer appeared in the ebony sky, she realized that David had the Singer back and, under her nephew's stewardship, the miracle crystal had done its job. The magical crystal that she had discovered on one of her archeological digs and gave to her nephew - knowing he was the Singer's rightful owner - had worked miracles for everyone she loved.

With a shaky hand, Dorothy signed upward to the heavens, "I'm ready to go home." Then she closed her eyes, and in that ethereal knowing that comes with the imminence of death, she knew her family would be all right. Taking one last breath of life, Dorothy drifted off peacefully to her next incarnation.

* * *

On the first morning of the New Year, David visits his sister in the hospital. She is sleeping peacefully, and without waking her, he is finally able to do what he longed to do since returning home: place the Rose Crystal Pendant around her neck.

When Sally's eyes flutter open and she speaks to him, David cannot hear his sister's voice. He doesn't need to, for he can read her lips. It is something he knows he will have to do the rest of his life, for he gave up his ability to hear so that Sally could be cured. She will never know the sacrifice he made for her. According to his doctor the cochlear implant inexplicably failed. A rare, but not unheard of, occurrence.

"Can you help me get up out of this bed?"Sally asks her big brother. "I can't stand lying here another minute."

David holds her arm as Sally slowly gets out of bed and stands on her own two feet. When she takes wobbly but promising steps, he knows he has made the right decision, the only decision.

"Are you okay, Sal? Is it too soon for you to get up and walk? Don't rush it."

"Yes, I'm good. And no, it's not too soon. Mom said it was about time."

"Mom?" David looks at her, puzzled.

"Yeah. I had the strangest dream about Mom. I mean I think it was a dream. It was so real. I could see and feel her just like she was here in this room."

"Really? What did she say?"

"She said she came to say goodbye, and didn't want us to be sad or hurt anymore. I really got the feeling she meant it was time I stopped being a pitiful cripple and get up and walk again. Weird, huh?"

"Yeah. Weird."

"It's okay that you can't hear, David," Sally adds. "If you can hear in that other world and that makes you happy, then I'm happy, too."

Surprised by her words, David asks, "Why do you think I can still go to that 'other world' and can hear there?"

Sally touches the glistening pendant around her neck. "Because you found the Rose Crystal."

Thirty-eight

At the Nickerson home, the family makes arrangements for Dorothy's funeral. They read her will and discover she has bequeathed her sloop *Moonsinger* to David. Her wish is that she be cremated and her ashes spread in the ocean beneath the cliff of the family cemetery. All she wants in the family plot is a small stone with a photo of her aboard the sloop, and the inscription: "To my beloved Isaac, Sally and David. Thank you for a glorious life journey. May yours be as smooth sailing as mine has been."

For Isaac, having his daughter completely well is more than he could have ever hoped for. But along with that precious gift, he is finally able to put his feelings for Billie to rest. The guilt he suffered over her fatal accident has finally been assuaged. The car crash was fate. There was nothing he did to cause it and nothing he could have done to prevent it. This revelation surprises him, but he welcomes the relief from the nagging hurt.

So, Isaac and Janice finally set a wedding date - to be married on the exact day that they celebrate Dorothy's life.

"I want to spend the rest of my life with you, Jan," Isaac declares, placing the engagement ring back on her finger. "And I want it to begin now, as soon as possible."

"So do I, Isaac. But tell me, why the hurry when you've been so hesitant to set a specific date?"

"I had this very vivid dream recently that Billie came to me and told me it was time to move on with my life, with you, and stop feeling guilty about her death. She was so right. And I want our wedding to be something special."

What could be more special than a wedding aboard the beautiful, sleek Miracle Ship that Isaac had designed and that he and Janice had raised millions of dollars to fund. Yes, it had been badly damaged in one of Ramirez's self-created storms, but an anonymous benefactor donated the money for its repair so it would be ready in time to be used for Isaac and Janice's humanitarian cause – and for their wedding voyage.

But it's all bittersweet for David. He is overjoyed that Sally can walk again, that the Rose Crystal worked its magic and healed her body, mind and soul. But he cannot forget the promise he had also made to his aunt, that he would find a way to get her well, to have her recover fully from her stroke. With a heavy heart he must bid farewell to her, in a ceremony of her choosing. *Did she also choose the time and circumstances of her death? Like mom did? Or the way I chose my deafness?* David wonders. *Could I have even done anything to help her? Was it my place, part of my mission?*

Obviously not.

On a brisk sunny January morning, David, Sally, Isaac and Janice board a small pilot boat that will take them to the Miracle Ship. From this little boat that bobs joyfully beneath the cliff where the Nickerson family cemetery stands, David scatters Dorothy's ashes in the calm water. Secretly in the palm of his hand is the Singer, and as the ashes spill from the urn, David lets the crystal slip into the sea with his aunt's remains.

She was the one who found it and gave it to me, David muses. *Maybe it will bring her happiness in a whole new life. If she wants me to have it again, it will find its way back to me. She'll see to that...*

"It's called a Singer," Dorothy had said those many months ago, signing the word *Singer*, referring to the boat-shaped gem she had discovered on one of her archaeological digs abroad.

"Why do they call it that?"

"Each crystal in the cluster contains its own unique vibration," she told him, "but joined together like this they create a symphony of sounds that literally sing the answers to all the mysteries in the universe. Or so the legend goes."

"I bet it's thousands, maybe millions of years old," David figured.

The crystal sparkled pure and translucent one minute, a rainbow mosaic the next, a jigsaw arrangement of atoms, a harmonic conversion of energy and matter. Yet, it looked amazingly like a primitive sculpture fashioned by someone in love with the sea.

"It's incredible. Look at it, Aunt Dorothy. Its microstructure is so complex. But what really amazes me is its shape. It looks like a miniature ship. Here's the mast where the sail would go, and here's the bow, the stern and the rudder."

Dorothy added more impetus to the Singer's mystique. The crystal was destined to have but one owner, or so the legend went. "If its owner believes in it, and works with its energy, he will develop extraordinary powers of communication, clairvoyance and prophecy..."

As important as his ownership of the Singer has been, affording him amazing gifts through what he had considered his "disability," he realizes now that it was also his vehicle to self-discovery. For some it is found in prayer or meditation. But for David, his silent world has been made audible and meaningful through the power of this precious crystal. His mission is now complete. His mother is at peace, his father is happy and successful, his sister has been healed of her infirmity, and Port Avalon is safe and secure.

Thirty-nine

Onboard the Miracle Ship, preparations are being made for Isaac's and Janice's wedding. The deck and salon are lushly adorned with lilies, orchids and tulips in red, white and yellow. A wedding cake in the shape of the Nickerson family's historic Victorian home is splendidly iced in white cream, with a rooftop and shutters fashioned out of fresh red edible flowers. The ship's crew wears winter white suits with red boutonnières, with the Captain in full dress as the officiator of the ceremony.

Heather, who has been ferried over for the wedding festivities, giggles with delight along with Sally over their dusty rose colored silk organza bridesmaid dresses and helps Janice with the elegant floral spray in her shiny ebony hair fashioned in a beautiful ribboned braid.

There is no need for David to help Isaac with a bow tie, for he has opted instead for a cool blue silk tunic and white pants as a complement to Janice's ice blue linen sheath.

David wears the blue monogrammed shirt that his mother made for him, the one he wore to visit her at the cemetery where he went to talk with her, to find out why she died and left him all alone.

Just as now, it had been a day of celebration as well as a day of mourning...

Isaac, David and Sally laid flowers on Billie Nickerson's grave and after some sentimental tears and memories, they then enjoyed a dinner at their favorite restaurant on Lighthouse Point to celebrate what would have been Isaac's and Billie's wedding anniversary.

But sullen and maudlin, David needed more from his mother that day. He needed to actually talk with her. Listening to his Aunt Dorothy who suggested David needed to get back to working with his crystals again, he gathered them up along with the Singer and headed for the cemetery. In front of his mother's grave stone, he paced back and forth, kicked up some loose dirt, and teetered back and forth on his heels.

Finally David blurted out, "Why is this so hard. All I want to do is talk to – " David choked on the words. "Just talk to you, Mom. But how do I know you can hear me now? You didn't hear me in the hospital when I begged you not to die. Maybe you don't want to. Maybe it's so great where you are that you don't want to know about us anymore. You don't want to know about our problems and how much we need you. Is that it? Did you get tired of being needed so much, of always having us on you about something? Mom, fix my lunch. Mom, ask Dad if I can stay out late tonight. Mom, I'm not a kid anymore. Leave me alone…leave me alone…"

David dropped to his knees and cried all the tears he hadn't let himself cry for months, rivers of tears, flowing in torrents, so many tears that his eyes swelled up and his nose ran. He wiped it with the back of his hand.

"Damn it! Why didn't you listen to me," he had yelled, pounding the ground with his fist. "Do you have any idea what's happened since you left? Dad nearly died himself from the guilt. Sally's legs are useless. And me - I'm a mess. I don't know what happened to me. I went to some strange place on this mystery ship and had all kinds of insane things happen - a storm, and monsters, and…and all kinds of wonderful things, too. There was a girl there. I think I loved her and I think she loved me…

"Mom, I could hear there. I could hear everything, but I don't understand how or why. And I can't talk to anybody about it. Not Dad or Aunt Dorothy, though she'd understand probably more than anybody. Not to Sally - she'd believe anything I said, she believes in me so much. But I let them both down. I don't have any special gifts," he sobbed softly, "except in my dreams. The worst part is that I'm so mad all the time. Aunt Dorothy thinks I'm mad at you. She told me to come here today, to talk to you about my crystals, and maybe I'd stop being so mad."

David removed his crystals from the silk pouch and laid them out on the grave by the headstone in the mystical Star of David gridwork pattern with the Singer crystal at the apex.

"The last time I did this, I was taken far away. Maybe I can do it again. Only this time, I want to be with you, Mom. I want to see you face to face again so I can understand why you left and what I have to live for!"

The relentless sun bore down on the cemetery and on Billie Nickerson's grave. The Singer glinted and sparkled, creating a glare so strong that David had to shield his eyes.

Encased in a mantle of white light, obscuring his view of everything around him, David heard a soft hum that built to a frequency so shrill he squeezed his hands over his ears. The unbearable tenor persisted and David protectively pulled out his hearing aid. But instead of total silence, the piercing tone became a celestial voice, unlike anything David could ever imagine, sweeter even than Saliana's song. David looked up and the marble angel guarding his mother's grave was with him in the light. He swore she was singing to him. In the intense, blinding radiance, the angel's wing cracked as though struck by a bolt of lightning.

The vision before him was more than David could comprehend, holographic at first, an image from a distant dimension, shimmering and ephemeral. But a vision so warm, so embracing that David moved toward it, willingly, longingly, unafraid. It took shape, form, content. Her gold hair moved freely in the gentle wind. She was more lovely, more serene, than he'd ever seen her. Had it not been for the dress, David would not have been so certain who she was. The pink sheath, the one she made, the one they buried her in, caressed her body demurely. She was vibrant, breathtaking, alive, and her touch was real. And she spoke:

"I'm here, David. I'm here. I will always be here, though you won't always know me. Take the journey, David. Take the journey and I will take it with you..."

That was months ago, before David's transport to Coronadus on the Moon Singer, and before he met Bianca, his Mother's spirit image; before he discovered the Wind Rose in the Coronadus Emporium, the mystical compass that magically brought to life a city that was caught in a windless, stagnant time warp.

That was months ago, before he had any notion of why he was chosen - *or did he choose?* - to allow his life to intertwine with the lives of others on planes of existence that most people believe are merely a fantasy. In doing so he came to know that karmic debts actually are accrued, that the decisions one makes in one moment have a rippling effect on every moment thereafter.

Forty

The gleaming white Miracle Ship, in David's mind an earthly clone of the Moon Singer that transported him to amazing times and places, is now fully staffed with volunteer physicians, medical personnel and supplies, engineers and agricultural workers, and rehabilitation equipment. It will travel the globe to bring medical care, surgeries and medicines to thousands of people in disadvantaged and remote countries who would otherwise die from lack of even basic health care and vaccinations. The volunteers will help to build schools, clinics and orphanages, and dig water wells to provide a village with water for the very first time.

But on this day, it is time to celebrate new beginnings, the marriage of Janice Cole to Isaac Nickerson.

After the sweet and brief ceremony, lots of food, music and dancing - and Sally *really* dancing, not just being carried along by her brother - David and Heather take a walk on the inside deck, rekindling their friendship.

The turning point for David came when Heather, now a bit more assertive about where their relationship is going, told him he needed to open up a bit more, to be available to love. Perhaps the romance of the wedding, and the fact that his family is now happy and hopeful, allows David himself to feel serene enough to contemplate a relationship with someone.

They walk around the beautiful white polished decks, aglow with thousands of tiny lights strung across the banisters. The moon is high and silvery in the sky, visible through the spotlessly clean windows.

"I'd really like to have the kind of relationship my dad and my mom had. Where do you find someone like that, you know, a real soul mate?"

"You know David," Heather reminds him, signing that he is to look at her face, "love is right under your nose, but you can't see it."

David stops in his tracks. "That's what Saliana said."

"Who's Saliana?"

"Huh? Oh. Just someone I ... once knew... someone who helped me see that I should appreciate what's right here at home."

"Smart girl. I'd like to meet her," Heather says, trying hard not to be jealous of some unknown woman.

"Well, she's gone now," David reassures her. "I doubt I'll see her again."

Heather smiles. "Good."

"I'm not so sure it's good," David replies wistfully. "She was a very important part of my life."

"Do you want to talk about it?" Heather asks, her heart fluttering with nervousness, as they walk on.

"It's too complicated. I'm not sure I could explain it, how we met and what we meant to each other."

"This sounds serious. Are you sure you're over her?"

"Truthfully? No...I'm not sure."

Heather stops short and grabs David's arm. "David Nickerson!" Heather says, signing emphatically every word she announces out loud. "You tell me right now if I mean anything to you, if we have any kind of future together or if I should just move on!"

David put his hands gently on her shoulders, trying to reassure her. "No, no. You do mean something to me, Heather. It's just that I never know what's going to happen to me. My life has been so crazy."

"Crazy? You mean like walking on water and getting on a clipper ship made of crystal and gold and then sailing through the air out of sight? That kind of crazy?"

David drops his hands to his sides, slightly embarrassed. "Well...yeah...that is crazy all right."

"Are you ever going to explain that to me?"

David is stumped. He wants to tell her, but then again doesn't want to. It's his personal experience, his very own manifestation. Yet, he needs to tell someone all of it.

Not today, however.

"Be patient with me, Heather," David says. "I might be able to tell you someday. But if I did, you'd probably run for the hills. I don't want to lose you over this."

Heather sighs deeply. "I know I'll be sorry for letting you off the hook, but it's okay. I'll try to wait for someday."

Epilogue

Sally deftly climbs the steep, narrow stairs to the attic of the house. From the top of the stairs, David smiles happily at his sister's agility.

"Did you find the chest, David?" Sally moves her fingers swiftly to sign the question.

"No," he says, clearing away some cobwebs from the rafters. "I waited for you so we could make this mysterious discovery together."

David and Sally carefully move and re-stack boxes and old furniture to another part of the attic to reveal the secretly stored chest Dorothy bequeathed to them.

"I wonder why no one ever found it before now."

"I don't know that anybody even knew it was up here but Aunt Dorothy," David reminds her. "No one's been up here in years."

"It looks almost new, even though it's an antique."

Using the oversized key Dorothy had put in the envelope with a copy of her Will, David easily opens the teakwood treasure chest. He lifts the lid and rests it back on its hinges. Inside are other small boxes and items wrapped in silk cloth, mementos of Dorothy's colorful life as a member of the Nickerson clan.

One by one, Sally and David carefully open each box, reveal each photo. One in particular catches Sally's attention. It is a sepia-toned photo of a beautiful woman, dressed rather glamorously in a satin and lace form-fitting gown. It is signed, just as one would sign an autograph, "To my beloved grandniece, Dorothy. Welcome to the world. Love, your Aunt Rose."

In the same package as the photo, there are theater playbills featuring the name Rose Wyndham, as "chanteuse and principal dancer" in several turn-of-the-century shows.

"David, this was Dorothy's aunt? That means she was Dorothy's mother's sister, and our great aunt? She sang and danced, and her name was Rose. How amazing."

"More than amazing, Sal. Take a closer look at what's around her neck."

Sally gasps. "My gosh!" She instinctively places her hand up to her chest, where the Rose Crystal pendant rests. "It looks just like — "

"Just like," David repeats.

"This is so exciting, David. What else are we going to find?"

"Well, I have a feeling the answers are in here." David holds up an old journal and opens the cover.

Inside is a picture of an old man, David and Sally's great-grandfather, standing on the deck of a beautiful white sailing ship. He squints to make out the name imprinted on the hull, but it is too small. Sally hands David a magnifying glass that is packed inside the journal's box. He holds it close to the picture and lets the image clarify. One by one, David reads the letters, "W – i – n – d"

"Golly, David. It can't be…"

"It is. It's called The Wind Rose."

David and Sally settle in comfortably, ready to discover all the secrets and connections their lives hold to the past, how they are affecting the present, and hopefully where they will lead them in the future.

* * *

Later, in David's Room, Isaac visits his son and sees the Wind Rose compass. He picks it up and studies it carefully.

"David, where did you get this?"

"It's a long story, a really long story."

"I'm ready to listen, son. Let's take a walk together."
"Sure, Dad. I'd like that."

* * *

"And so, his journey ends."
Other: For now.
"With a powerful realization."
Other: That the ability to know, understand and make meaningful choices is within all of us. No one can do it for us. Yet we do not do it alone.

"We can seek guidance, look to role models for advice, but in the end the choice is ours - in this case *his* - alone."
Other: Accept gratefully the consequences and the rewards.

The End

Dear reader,

We hope you enjoyed reading *The Wind Rose*. Please take a moment to leave a review, even if it's a short one. Your opinion is important to us.

Discover more books by B. Roman at
https://www.nextchapter.pub/authors/b-roman

Want to know when one of our books is free or discounted? Join the newsletter at http://eepurl.com/bqqB3H

Best regards,
B. Roman and the Next Chapter Team

Author Notes

Since childhood, I've been torn between two worlds: writing and singing. It's difficult to serve "two masters," as they say, but I was compelled to do so. When I was not singing, I was writing; when I was not writing, I was singing. Now I do both. (While still working a day job!)

I've learned, for me, that one creative expression nurtures the other. Much of my writing has a musical theme somewhere in the plot, or is the plot, whether it's in my non-fiction writing about the power of music itself, in picture books and stories, and of course in writing songs and lyrics for songs.

It is natural, therefore, that my trilogy of adventures for young readers, "The ~~Secrets of the~~ Moon Singer," has its roots in musical theories and metaphors, entwined with the magic and mystery of metaphysical concepts and matters of ethics, faith, compassion, love, and heroism. Books 1 and 2 of my trilogy lay the groundwork for this power of music of the highest order. Book 3 pulls it all together and will give you a complete understanding of the importance of music in our lives and in the world.

Most of all, I hope my books inspire you to know that, whatever your circumstances in life - just as my "hero" David Nickerson learns - your greatest challenges are opportunities for growth and strength, and that your "disability," if you have one, can be your greatest gift.

I've lived a long life (won't tell you how long!), and my path has gone every which way but straight to my goals, but I believe that my time for soul fulfillment is NOW. Perhaps my books will inspire that belief in you as well.

B Roman, Author

The Wind Rose
ISBN: 978-4-86752-751-1

Published by
Next Chapter
1-60-20 Minami-Otsuka
170-0005 Toshima-Ku, Tokyo
+818035793528
9th August 2021

Lightning Source UK Ltd.
Milton Keynes UK
UKHW012331250821
389480UK00001B/136